GRIDIRON CRUSADER

Westminster Press Books by

DICK FRIENDLICH

Warrior Forward
Line Smasher
Play Maker
Baron of the Bull Pen
Left End Scott
Clean Up Hitter
Gridiron Crusader

GRIDIRON CRUSADER

by

DICK FRIENDLICH

PHILADELPHIA

THE WESTMINSTER PRESS

Library of Congress Catalog Card No. 58–10330

PRINTED IN THE UNITED STATES OF AMERICA

1

ED SAVAGE looked at his wrist watch as he walked along the side lines.

"One more series, Whites, and we'll knock off," he shouted to the cluster of footballers in grass-stained sweat shirts. "Let's see if you can get six before we quit."

He turned toward the bench and said in a lower voice: "Two hours are plenty, don't you think, Sam? Some of the kids are beginning to fade."

"Righto. That's when a boy can get hurt — when he's bushed."

Sam LaCosta was short and stocky, a good four inches under Savage's six feet. Like Ed, he wore a black-visored baseball cap, sweat shirt, and lightweight football pants. But where Savage was narrow-waisted, with broad shoulders and long, stringily-muscled legs, LaCosta, built along the lines of a fire hydrant, bulged muscularly from calf to chest.

Savage glanced at the list of names fastened to the clip board in his hand. There was at least one check mark against each of the fifty-six names on the list, signifying that the person had played at least fifteen minutes in this game-style scrimmage which ended six weeks of spring practice for the Cavaliers of Hastings University.

5

As the new head coach, Savage wanted a look at every one of the varsity candidates, from the probable first stringers to the earnest youths who lacked size, speed, or agility, or all three, and had only desire to recommend them. He had worked harder with the last group these past six weeks than with the natural athletes. At Niles College where Savage had spent the last two pleasantly successful years, his squads had been long on desire and the will to win and short on inherent ability, but they had lost only two games in two seasons.

At a small school like Niles, Ed thought, the will to win was sometimes enough. But not at Hastings. This was the big league. Savage knew that from experience. He had played in it, not so long ago.

The May sun was hot. Savage took off his cap and wiped a thin band of perspiration from his forehead. With his close-cropped blond hair and his tanned, unlined face, he looked not much older than many of the players in his charge. And in fact he was not.

Ed Savage was twenty-six. As a Hastings halfback five years before, he had run the length of this same practice field times beyond count. Portly, gray-haired Pappy Wilkins had been Hastings' coach then. But Pappy was gone, after eighteen years as head man, and so was Jim Trainor, his successor, and now he, Edward Gordon Savage, was in charge of Cavalier football.

Those five years seemed much longer, a lifetime compressed in themselves. The quick step from Commencement Day exercises to the Air Force uniform; the nightmare of fighter missions over Korea; the brief, one-season career in professional football cut short by knee injury; and then the two years of coaching in friendly, unpressured fashion at the small Midwest school called Niles.

More than once in the past three months, Savage had

6

awakened at night with the hazy feeling that he had dreamed most of it, that somehow time had run together and he was still a student at Hastings.

But it was not a dream. For reasons that Savage still did not understand fully, Cal Murchison, the Cavaliers' director of athletics, had plucked him from obscurity. Jim Trainor, brought in to give Hastings a winning team, had failed, and was allowed to resign after four seasons unsatisfactory to students, alumni, and administration alike.

Savage had had no idea that Murchison could even recall his name. He had not set foot on the Hastings campus since graduation. But Murchison had telephoned him and offered him the job, and when Ed had been convinced that he was not the butt of some practical joke, he had somewhat dazedly accepted.

He would never be able to discharge his debt to Murchison, he told himself many times. He could only try to turn out a team that would wear the red and white with honor, win or lose.

The white-shirted center came up over the ball, and the defense, wearing distinguishing sleeveless red pullovers, began to chatter noisily. Involuntarily, Savage's gaze swung to the strapping 220-pounder in the center of the red secondary — Vince Crump, the middle line backer. There was a football player, Ed thought. Big, fast, and smart, a fellow who liked the rough going. Sometimes Savage thought Crump liked it a little too much. He had an uneasy feeling about Vince.

Glass, the Whites' quarterback, chanted the signals in a high, squeaking voice. Then he turned and took three steps to his right, moving along with the fullback slanting outside tackle and putting the ball into his cradled arms. The fullback picked the hole deftly and quick-stepped through it, head low, body bent at the waist.

But the fullback didn't have the ball. Both he and Glass had faked neatly on this "holdout" play. Glass had kept the ball and now he was running right and shoveling it swiftly out to Scarsella, the left half, who had come around behind the fullback and was swinging wide outside the defensive end.

"Now scramble!" Savage shouted. The slim Scarsella sprinted toward the side line, then turned the corner just beyond the grasp of the Reds' outside line backer.

The defensive halfback drifted back warily, trying to pinch the runner against the side line as other red-shirts bore down from behind. Scarsella made two feints, then attempted to cut back to the inside.

The red halfback did not buy either feint, and as Scarsella made the turn, he dove for the runner's legs, wrapping his arms tightly around one of them.

Scarsella, still upright and twisting and turning on his free leg, dragged the tackler forward perhaps another yard before George Breck, an assistant coach serving as referee, blew the whistle to end the play.

At the whistle's blast, Scarsella and the tackler both relaxed. A split second later, a red-shirted form flashed through the air and smashed Scarsella from the side with a fearful impact.

"Jupiter!"

The word burst angrily from Savage's lips, and he started across the field at top speed. Even from that distance, he knew that the man who had felled Scarsella in such needless fashion was Vince Crump. He knew, also, with a sinking feeling, that the halfback was not going to get up.

⌒

Savage sat on a bench in the gym locker room, cap in hands, trying to appear amiable. But there was a troubled look in his gray eyes as he submitted to the questions of the two newspapermen, young Roy Caster, sports editor of the college daily, and Jake Gledhill, from the *Tribune*.

Gledhill, a stout, rumpled-looking man of middle age, had been on the *Tribune* for years, and Ed knew him from his own playing days. The sports writer had welcomed him warmly as coach, in person as well as in print in his daily column, "Everything's Jake." Savage had reason to be grateful to Gledhill.

But now Gledhill was seeking a statement on the injury to Joe Scarsella, and Savage, against all his natural inclinations, tried to evade making the direct answer. It cut across the grain of his innate honesty not to answer the question as truthfully as he could. But first he wanted a word with Vince Crump, and he had not yet had that opportunity.

"Jake, it's a knee, but Doc Beardsley can't tell whether it's just a bruise or something's torn until he sees the X rays. We'll know tomorrow."

Gledhill grunted and took an empty pipe from his mouth. He peered shrewdly at Savage through horn-rimmed spectacles, looking like an untidy owl.

"Do you think Breck was a little slow on the whistle, Ed? Or was Crump a little overeager? Seemed to me he took off on Joe after the whistle. You have that impression?"

Savage winced inwardly, but mustered a look of surprise. Those questions had been revolving in his own mind for half an hour.

"No, Jake! It was just one of those things. George was quick enough with the whistle, but Crump didn't hear it. You know how a fellow can miss it in the excitement of a game."

"This wasn't a game, just a scrimmage," the sports

9

writer said mildly. " I wonder why Vince tries to knock himself out — to say nothing of others — in scrimmage."

Savage shot a covert glance at Roy Caster, wondering if the student sports editor, who had remained respectfully silent as Gledhill conducted the interview, divined what Jake was driving at.

" Vince always plays that way, I'm told," Ed said, frowning slightly. " He's been a real hard knocker all spring."

" Jim Trainor picked a lot of hard knockers, if you haven't noticed," Gledhill said in a dry voice. " Well, I'll check the doc tomorrow on Scarsella. Now, did you like what you saw today, and if not, why not, and where will Hastings finish in the Big Eight? "

The somewhat strained look around Savage's eyes vanished. He almost laughed in relief at this turn to the routine line of questioning. There were standard answers, too, especially for a new coach, as young and inexperienced as he.

He answered diplomatically, pointing out that he had only had this past six weeks to work with a group he had never seen before, and that wasn't long enough for firm predictions. He had been favorably impressed with the showing of this boy and that one, but there was still a lot to be done before the Cavaliers would be ready for a game with anyone.

" By George, you sound just like every other coach I've ever talked to," Gledhill said. He had not taken a note, but Caster had made hurried notes as Savage talked. " You wouldn't concede that today is Saturday without qualifying that it might be Friday. Do you think you'll win more games than Trainor did last year? "

He slipped the last question in swiftly, and Savage grinned at him.

"I'm green, Jake," he replied, gray eyes twinkling, "but I'm really hurt that you think I'm green enough to give an answer to that one."

Hastings had won three games, lost six the previous season, including the Rossiter game for the third successive year. That had finished Trainor.

"I may quote you exactly on that," Jake said blandly. "In a way, it's kind of revealing."

He made a gesture to Caster indicating the field was clear, and the student plunged in eagerly.

"How about a first-string line-up, Coach? As of now, I mean."

"Sure, Roy," Savage said tolerantly, "but it's really not much more than a guess. By October 1, it may be eleven other fellows."

That wasn't strictly true, because he knew he had no better guard than Crump, nor had he a better tackle than Larry Hearst, from the frosh, looked to be right now. And Junior Travis was the ideal T-formation halfback — quick off the mark, a hard driver, good blocker and pass receiver. But no one, not even Crump, was going to think he had a job sewed up in May.

He went through the line-up slowly.

"And fullback — well, let's say Freeman, though it could be Schmidt or Olvera just as well," he concluded. "That do it?"

Gledhill studied the list he'd written.

"Travis at half, eh?" he asked, as though talking to himself.

"I think so. Surprise you?" There was something odd in Jake's voice, Savage thought, puzzled.

"No. Only Jim didn't seem to think much of him. He was third or fourth string last year."

It was on the tip of Savage's tongue to say that if

11

Trainor had two better halfbacks than Junior Travis last year, Hastings shouldn't have lost six games. But he did not dwell on it, for he was impatient to talk to Crump before the player left the building.

To his relief, Gledhill did not pursue the subject, and the interview trickled to an end. As the writers left, Savage strode quickly across the corridor to the other side of the gym, which housed the gridmen's dressing rooms.

Only a few players remained, but Crump was one of them, in a group of four. He was not the tallest — Hearst, the six-foot, four-inch tackle, topped him by three inches, and Whitney, an end, by two — but to Savage he appeared much the biggest.

Perhaps it was Crump's width of chest and shoulder, or the solid column of his neck that jutted out of his sports shirt. Perhaps it was the confident manner in which he carried himself; standing there rocking gently on his heels, hands thrust into the pockets of his slacks, he radiated assurance.

Under his black hair, glistening from the recent shower, Crump's face was strong-jawed and square. His teeth showed white against his dark complexion, and a thin, light scar, perhaps the width of a pencil, lay along one cheek. A sniper's bullet in Korea had done that, for Vince Crump was only a year younger than Savage. Jim Trainor had brought him to Hastings as a freshman under the GI bill.

"Come on, Big Dog," Hearst said impatiently as Savage approached. "You want to hang around here all day?"

"Easy, Larry, easy," Crump said lazily. "There's nothing worth hurrying for. Not at my age. You'll learn."

"You talk like a man a hundred and twelve, Big Dog," Whitney snickered. "Larry's right. It's a good fifty miles

12

and we ought to get there before seven. Come on."

Keeping his tone casual, Savage said, " Vince, come here a minute, will you? "

The group turned toward him. Crump said: " Wait for me outside. Coach wants to talk to me."

Annoyance flickered briefly in Savage's gray eyes. All the players called him " Coach," but Crump gave it a drawling undertone in which Savage thought he could detect a hint of mockery. It was as though Vince was informing listeners that there was really not very much the coach could tell him that he didn't already know.

" O.K., Big Dog," Whitney said. " How'd we do today, Coach? "

" I'll let you know after I see the pictures," Savage said amiably, and thought to himself that Whitney had too flip an attitude, as if he was aping Crump. " I seem to remember you missing a block on the halfback. Right out in front of everybody, too."

" I'm saving my good ones for the regular season," the end replied impudently, and with Hearst and Gannon, the other member of the quartet, strolled into the corridor.

Savage glanced around quickly. He did not want this conversation overheard. Sam LaCosta was talking to Murchison near the entrance to the shower room, and George Breck was helping two student managers stow away equipment. Otherwise the room was empty.

" Vince, I know you didn't hear the whistle on the last play, but didn't you see that Scarsella was stopped? We don't have so many halfbacks that we want 'em killed by our own men, you know."

" No one's sorrier about Joe than I am," Crump said firmly. " I left my feet and then the whistle blew, and I couldn't turn aside in time. But you're mistaken about Joe

13

being stopped. He was still on his feet and going for extra yards, and I figure you're entitled to hit a man when he's doing that."

His heavy-lidded eyes regarded Savage steadily as he spoke, and Ed felt a sense of frustration. Crump's straightforward reply had thrown him on the defensive. Of course, a player was supposed to put out just as hard in practice as he would in a game. It was one of the first tenets of coaching.

"Well, try not to mangle any more than you can help," he said feebly. Crump smiled a little.

"Will do. Anything else, Coach?"

"No, that was all, Vince."

I didn't make any dent in him, Savage thought with a vague feeling of defeat. Well, time enough to work it out in the fall.

"Ed, why so solemn? Aren't you pleased about the scrimmage? I am, believe me!"

Cal Murchison's voice boomed across the room. Savage crossed toward him, conscious of a surge of affection for the man who had, almost singlehanded, been responsible for his appointment.

Murchison was tall and spare and stood straight as a plumb line. Although his hair was pure white, he wore it crew cut, and it gave him a youthfully jaunty air.

"It wasn't too bad, I guess," Savage conceded. "I feel terrible about Scarsella, though. It looks like a bad knee."

"Aw, don't let that depress you, Ed." Murchison gave his shoulder a friendly squeeze. "Football's a contact game — who should know better than you? Anyway, no one can tell about knees right away; Joe will probably be all right by fall. But I thought it was a smasher of a workout, truly, and so did the alumni I talked to. They liked that flanker T stuff, and the way the linemen charged."

14

"That's Sam's department, the linemen," Savage said with a grin. He had persuaded LaCosta, who had been his line coach at Niles, to accompany him to Hastings, and he was glad to see him given credit for a good job. LaCosta was the only assistant of Savage's own choosing. Breck had been one of Trainor's aids, while Babe Bassich, the frosh coach, was a fixture of years' standing who withstood all changes at a higher level. He had coached Savage as a freshman.

LaCosta said in an amiable growl: " I'm only in charge of the linemen who charge straight ahead. George handles all the cross blocking and Ed supervises the stunting."

" What about the ends? " Murchison asked, amused.

" Oh, we just let them develop naturally. The Savage system, it's called. Very radical."

Murchison laughed outright.

" Sam didn't think our ends were much good today," Savage said, giving the line coach a playful shove. " I'm afraid he was right. But I did see a few things I liked."

" So did John Travis," Cal said heartily. " And I don't think it was just seeing Junior look good, either. He told me it was the best spring windup he'd watched in ten years."

Savage was pleased, though he considered the appraisal rather extravagant. John Travis was one of Hastings' most energetic alumni, who had helped send many athletes besides his son to his alma mater.

" Incidentally, Cal, what happened to young Travis last year? I understand he barely made his letter, but so far he looks like our best runner."

Murchison frowned slightly, but remained genial.

" Oh, Junior's a good runner, no argument. He and Jim just didn't hit it off. I'm happy to see him up there, frankly. John gives us a lot of help, as you know, and he was beginning to go just a leetle sour about the lad sitting on the bench."

Savage could understand that. He knew, though, that Murchison didn't expect Junior Travis to play first string just because his father carried a lot of water as an alumnus. Cal let the coach run the team. Otherwise, Travis would have played more than he did for Trainor.

"By the way, you two," Murchison said, "if you're free tonight, why not come by the house? Any time after eight. I'm having a few people in, nothing formal. You know some of them, I think."

LaCosta sent Savage a quick, inquiring look.

"Thanks, Cal," Ed said in embarrassment. "Fact is, I have an engagement. Any other time, I'd like to come."

"I'll have to scratch too, I'm afraid," LaCosta said apologetically. "I've been planning for the last two weeks to celebrate the end of practice."

The athletic director appeared somewhat disappointed but said cheerfully: "Sure, sure, boys. Well, don't break too many training rules. Drop in to see me Monday, will you, Ed? I want to talk over your plans for the summer."

When he had gone, Savage eyed LaCosta with suspicion.

"Do you really have a date tonight?"

"You think I'm too ugly to get one?" Sam asked truculently, then smiled in sheepish fashion. "Truth is, I don't, but I didn't feel up to going to Cal's alone. I don't know the crowd."

With some concern, Savage said: "I can't say I blame you, Sam, but you know the coaching business. You have to mix now and then. I'm certainly not looking forward to the banquet circuit this summer, but it goes with the job."

"I know," LaCosta sighed, grimacing. "But when I can duck it gracefully, I will. Tonight I'm going to stay in our miserable little hovel and read a book. Shall I wait up for you, or do you really have an engagement, as you call it? "

Savage's ears reddened slightly.

" Yes, I do," he answered with more emphasis than necessary, and LaCosta grinned.

" La Fleming? "

" If you mean Sarah Fleming, yes," Ed said with dignity. " You want any more details, such as where we'll eat, anything like that? I could bring back a menu."

" Oh, no, no." LaCosta tried to look demure. " I was only concerned about your welfare, Ed."

" O.K.," Savage muttered. " She's a good kid. Besides, she's the only girl I know around here."

He did not add that he and Sarah Fleming had once talked of marriage. But that had been ages ago. Korea had been only a name on a map, and Savage had looked forward to four years of medical school. Now he and LaCosta shared a small house on the Hastings campus and they were close friends, but there were some things Savage discussed with no one. Not even with Sarah — now.

LaCosta, divining that he had pursued the subject about as far as it would go comfortably, turned serious.

" I saw you talking to Crump, Ed. Did you jack him up for that play on Scarsella? "

" No, I didn't." Savage spoke more sharply than he had intended. " He explained he was in mid-air and couldn't stop. Crump's one of those fellows who goes all out every minute. You've seen that kind before."

LaCosta's swarthy features were expressionless.

" Yeah, I've seen that kind. Well, me for the shower."

He began to pull off his sweat shirt. Savage, his eyes clouding, had the uncomfortable feeling of a man who had not quite measured up to expectations.

17

2

THE trouble with football coaches, I find," said Sarah Fleming, "is that they won't talk about football."

Savage blinked and put down his coffee cup. The girl across the table was smiling at him, a mischievous gleam in her brown eyes. She was small-boned, with a pert, oval face and black hair drawn straight back and coiled at the nape of her neck. She could not have been called beautiful, or even really pretty by conventional standards, but there was a gaiety about her and good humor that Savage had always found attractive. Five, six years before, she had worn her hair shoulder length, he remembered. Except for that, she did not seem to have changed at all in appearance. Had they danced, the top of her head would still have reached just to his shoulder.

" If that's a needle you're using on me, lady, it has a big square point," he said with a baffled look. " Frankly, I couldn't have picked a subject to interest you less. Or so I've been led to believe for a number of years."

" Ha! That's about on a par with the rest of your information about women, Mr. S.," she said tauntingly. " This is the third time we've been out, and except for a few grunts about professional football, you've not said a word about your work here. Not that I want you to diagram any

18

secret plays, but don't forget, I am not only a dues-paying member of the Hastings Alumni Association, but a member of the faculty as well. I have a right to know what the coach is thinking."

"Well, may I be dipped in chicken fat!" Savage said in genuine wonderment. "All right, Miss Alumna or Alumnae — I can never remember which is plural — where shall we start? The line or the backfield?"

She made a face at him.

"Let's start with the coach, shall we? Seriously, Ed, I'm terribly proud of you, being so successful so young."

She hesitated, and for a moment seemed at a loss. Then she said cheerfully: "But I remember your wanting so much to go to med school, wanting to be a good doctor, to help people. Of course, you went to war, but what happened to make you give up medicine and go back to football? Or should I keep my pointed nose out of your private affairs?"

"It's a very nice nose," Savage said, but his eyes were somber. The question had stirred memories, and not pleasant ones.

He supposed that it could be called fear. Well, perhaps just lack of courage, which was not quite the same thing. There had never been any money at all. He had come to Hastings on a scholarship — as a student, not an athlete. But because he was a football player, the athletic department had found him campus jobs and summer employment. He'd finished in the top tenth of his class, despite the long hours he had had to work, and he had saved enough at least to start him in medical school.

Savage remembered how he had looked forward to the challenge, because at that time being a doctor seemed all that mattered. Had there been no Korea, he would now be finishing his year as an intern, and somewhere there would be a sign reading " Edward Gordon Savage, M.D."

But he had lacked the courage to face those five years, to be pushing thirty when he would have to start earning a living. Things looked different to a youth of twenty-one than they did to a man of twenty-three with thirty-six missions behind him. It was not easy to explain.

" Nothing happened, Sarah," he said quietly, " except that I ran out of time. Assuming that I had the money to go to med school when I got out of the service — which I didn't — I'd be twenty-eight before I finished. I figured it was time I went to work, so when the Colts offered me a good chunk to play pro ball, I grabbed it. It was that simple. And it's turned out fine. Here I am, with one of the best jobs of its kind in the country, having dinner with the prettiest girl in the country. No, I'll amend that. Prettiest in the world, earth satellites included. Should I complain? "

Blushing, Sarah shook her head reprovingly.

" Flattery will get you somewhere, but not off this hook. It couldn't have been quite that simple in your mind. And it's a good mind, Ed."

She was in deadly earnest now, her eyes searching his face as though looking for an answer there.

" It's really too good a mind to waste on teaching boys to run up and down a field," she went on with a vehemence that startled Savage. " Oh, I know football is important and it's almost a science, but I think a man equipped to do something better ought to do it. Twenty years from now you'll be just like Cal Murchison."

The intensity of her feeling was unmistakable. The surprised Savage groped for a reply. Sarah gave a little sigh and spread her hands in a gesture of appeal.

" I suppose it's the schoolteacher in me," she offered

apologetically. " I really didn't mean to lecture you on how to run your life. Shall I leave quietly? "

Savage took a deep breath.

" We-e-ell! Not after that going-over, you don't leave. First, disregarding all that salve about my mind, I'm happy as a clam in my job. Sure, I wanted to be a doctor, and I have some regrets, but the circumstances didn't permit it and I made a choice I don't regret. You talk as though I'd gone into crime. Coaching is really quite respectable, young lady."

" I didn't say it wasn't," she protested, but he silenced her with a look he meant to be fierce.

" Furthermore, there's a good deal more to it than just running up and down a field, as you put it so kindly. I like working with kids. I think I can help them in many ways that have nothing to do with football. The way Pappy Wilkins helped me. If I didn't believe that, I'd be out of the business tomorrow. And lastly, what was that crack about Cal Murchison? He's one of the most respected men in college athletics, and I owe him a lot. My being here, for example."

Sarah looked as though she wished she had never mentioned the subject.

" Everyone says he's a fine man, Ed," she replied. " I certainly didn't mean to imply differently. But I knew his daughter Kitty, and she's told me her father was a brilliant law student here. He dropped out after a year to take a job with the athletic department — just temporarily, he thought — and he's still there. Certainly, he's head of the department and a big man in his field. I just happen to believe the field isn't important enough for someone with your brains. You ought to be using more than half of them. But if you're content, obviously I should never have opened my large mouth, and if you're still on speaking terms with me, I promise never again to mention your career. Friends? "

She extended her hand shyly.

"Friends, you little idiot," Ed said, grinning.

~

"And I must remind you," Savage said, his lean features quite serious, "that under state law, it is illegal to shoot a coach before September 15. Thank you."

He sat down as a ripple of laughter swept over the crowded banquet room. The chuckling gave way quickly to a round of enthusiastic hand clapping. Savage, flushing in appreciation, stared fixedly at the plate of unfinished and now melted ice cream before him. It was late August; he had given much the same speech a dozen times before Hastings alumni during the summer, and the applause never failed to stir him.

He was quite aware that it was not a personal tribute, but one offered to the head coach, whoever he might be. The same men cheering him now could just as noisily demand that he be fired if the Cavaliers lost their first few games. Which, he reminded himself, was entirely possible.

But for the moment, it was gratifying. Besides, he had caught a glimpse of Marty Regan's bulky form near the back of the room. Regan was football coach at Proctor Central High, long a breeding ground for future Hastings athletes. More important to Savage, though, was the memory of Marty as the blocking back who had cleared the path for him for two seasons in Pappy Wilkins' single-wing attack. Marty was an old friend; the prospect of seeing him again had given this trip to Proctor an added flavor.

Now the president of the alumni group, seated next to Savage, was rising to announce that the formal part of

22

the meeting was over, but that the head coach would be happy to talk with the members individually and answer questions.

The diners began to crowd up to the head table, and for the next half hour Savage was occupied with introductions and small talk. Happily, Marty Regan was among the first to reach him — a solidly built, black-haired Irishman with a deceptively sleepy look. Savage could not remember a more vicious blocker, but off the field Marty had been a gentle, even-tempered person who endured gibes and friendly horseplay with unfailing good nature.

" Hello, Biscuit Head," Savage greeted him. " You're getting fat as a goose."

Regan did not really look fat, but even after five years, Savage felt obliged to welcome him with some uncomplimentary remark. It was a way of saying that nothing had changed between them.

"It's the easy living does it, Eddie boy," Regan said. " Good to see you."

Speaking hurriedly, because of the others waiting to talk to him, Savage said: " I'm staying in the hotel overnight. Can you stick around, or maybe have breakfast with me tomorrow?"

Regan appeared to ponder the question.

Then he said slowly: " Well, sure. Tomorrow would be better. What time? "

" Make it nine. I'm in room 812. See you."

For a fleeting instant, Savage had an impression that Marty seemed a trifle reluctant to call on him. But he dismissed that as absurd as he turned to greet another alumnus, this one an extremely earnest citizen who wanted to show the coach a play that could not fail to gain at least ten yards every time.

23

"One thing about coaching in high school," Marty Regan said, "you don't have to mess with the alumni. Like that fish fry last night. You did it very smoothly, Ed, but I don't think you really enjoy it. Right?"

"Right." Savage patted the coffeepot tentatively, found it tepid, and desisted. He and Regan had been sitting in the hotel room for an hour, talking not about football, but about persons they'd known, trying to patch the gap in the years.

"I don't think anyone really enjoys the fried-chicken circuit, but it's an important part of the job and I knew it when I signed on. You'll do it, too, Marty, when the time comes."

Regan, slouched 'way down in a big chair, shook his head.

"Not me, sonny. I don't want a job coaching in college."

"You want to stay at Proctor all your life?" Savage asked in surprise. He recalled Regan as easygoing, but not without ambition.

"No, though it's a pleasant life. No recruiting, no alumni problems, as I said. But there isn't enough money in it for a family man. I'm interested in the administrative side — director of physical education, maybe even director of athletics. A college job, of course, but not as football coach. I've been going to summer school, getting my master's degree in phys. ed. In another two or three years, I'll be ready to leave here."

"Makes sense," Savage conceded. "An athletic director can fire the coach, but I never heard of one demanding his own resignation. You're smarter than you look, as we always claimed who were your friends. And that reminds me — recruiting. I know it's an ugly word at Hastings, but what about your boy Prindiville? I haven't heard from him

24

since he wrote me in June. No doubt about his coming next month, is there? "

Regan looked suddenly uncomfortable. He pulled his bulk erect in the chair.

" I suppose we had to come to Prindiville sooner or later," he said, and sighed. " Ed, the boy's not going to Hastings. I talked to him last week. He's enrolling at Burnside."

Savage was plainly astonished.

" Burnside? I don't understand, Marty. When I talked to him this spring, he was busting to come to Hastings. His grades are good; he's already applied and been admitted. What in the world happened? "

Regan rose abruptly. The troubled look in his eyes had deepened, and he had the air of a man about to embark on a distasteful task.

" Ed, you and I have known each other quite a while, even though we've been out of touch for years," he said heavily. " On that basis, I'm going to level with you, and maybe you won't think I'm your friend when I've finished.

" I didn't pressure Ted Prindiville in any way. He came to me last month and asked my advice — Hastings or Burnside. People had been talking to him; I don't know who. I told him that if he wanted to play football, I'd have to say Burnside. He won't learn any Jim Trainor tricks there — not from Dave Patterson. Dave is like Pappy was — play it tough, but play it clean."

For a moment, Savage could not believe he had heard correctly. Then he sprang to his feet, his face paling with anger.

" Trainor doesn't coach the Cavaliers any more." He bit off the words. " I do. I think you'd better make yourself clear."

25

"I'll try, Ed. I'm a Hastings man, and proud of it. The school stands for a lot of things to me — honorable things. First two years I was here, when I spotted a kid with guts and brains and character, I tried to sell him Hastings. You've got three of them now — Getsinger, Fairchild, and Bedolla.

"Two years ago I quit selling Hastings, because I didn't want my boys playing for Jim. He was brought out to produce a winner — which he didn't, but that's beside the point. But he figured anything went. I've watched Hastings players slug and knee and pile on, stunts that no coach should stand for. They've had more unnecessary roughness penalties than any other team in the league. I'll bet you didn't know that."

Savage had not known it, but before he could speak, Regan went on.

"Maybe I'm an idealist, but to me the game isn't a case of winning by crippling the other guy. Sure, a kid can lose his head in the heat of a game and take a swing at someone. But when the word goes around that any team playing the Cavaliers is in for a physical beating, win or lose, then it's time to get out. I got out."

He fell silent, gazing steadily at Savage.

"I've heard something about Jim's methods," Ed said in a thin tone. "I didn't know they were that bad. O.K., you didn't want your kids playing for him. Why don't you want them to play for me?"

"I saw your spring practice game, Ed," Regan said simply. "You've got a tough job, with a lot of Trainor's boys still there and one of his assistants on your staff. I don't know what luck you'll have making them change. That's about it."

The color began to return to Savage's face, though his mouth was a thin, hard line. At least, he thought bitterly,

Marty isn't accusing me of coaching dirty football. He just doesn't believe I'm strong enough to run the squad my way.

"Marty, I know you don't talk just to hear how you sound," he said, choosing his words with care, "but you're wrong on every count. I not only don't teach dirty football, I won't tolerate it. As for George Breck — well, I'm fairly new in the business. I didn't have a string of assistants ready to come with me. I brought the only good one I knew, Sam LaCosta. Breck is a first-class man; he wouldn't have any trouble finding another spot. He stayed because I asked him to, and we get along fine."

Regan, still looking unhappy, said: "I'm not belittling Breck's ability or suggesting that he'll undercut you, Ed. It's none of my business — until you ask about Prindiville. Then I either have to tell you the truth or think of some elaborate lie that won't hold up for long. Jim Trainor made a lot of Hastings men feel the same way I do. Some of them are coaches, as you'll discover for yourself."

The sense of outrage Savage had felt began to evaporate. He was shocked and hurt by Regan's attitude, but he could tell that Marty, for all his uncompromising honesty, felt bad about having to say what he thought.

"You were never one to box a man pretty, Marty," he said wryly. "I can't say I enjoyed this chat 100 per cent, but I understand your point of view. I think you'll change it. Come see our games, chum. We may not win, but we'll be clean, I promise you."

"I'll be there," Regan said.

On his return to the campus, Savage went at once to Murchison's office and gave Cal the outline of his talk with the Proctor coach. He did not mention the discussion of George Breck or references to himself. That was between him and Regan. But he believed the athletic

27

director should know of the feeling of disillusionment among some of the Old Reds.

To his surprise, Murchison was quite familiar with Regan's frame of mind. Nor was Cal so much disturbed as he was irritated.

"Marty's made no secret of his feelings," he said, frowning slightly. "Don't get upset about it. I regret it, naturally, because of the implication that we've made some compromise with our standards of sportsmanship.

"Do you honestly believe, Ed," Cal went on earnestly, "that I or any other responsible Hastings official would, for a single moment, stand for anything that even hinted of dirty football? Do you?"

"No, I don't." Regan has just been seeing things under the bed, Savage thought.

"Well, then." Murchison smiled. "Ed, I gave you the background when I offered you the job, but I left out some details. You know why Pappy had to resign. The Board wanted a winner. Too many alumni howling about Pappy's old-fashioned easy approach. I can tell you now that I opposed hiring Trainor, but I was overruled. They were looking for a tough guy, and they got him. Tough, mind you, nothing more.

"Jim brought some boys with him. I'm sorry to say that normally most of them would not have met our scholastic requirements for entrance. I dare say the Athletic Board regrets it now. Some of them are still on your squad. We'll fulfill our commitments to them until they graduate; we're honor-bound to do that. But from now on, we'll be what we were for twenty years — the hardest school to get into in the Big Eight."

Savage heard this with a growing sense of dismay. He knew the backgrounds and personal histories of his players, as much of them as he could absorb in the short

28

time he had been at Hastings. He knew which of them had been personally recruited by Trainor. But until now he had not realized that Hastings, in its scramble for a winning team, had gone so far as to slip football players in through the back door, if necessary.

Perhaps Murchison surmised what he was thinking, for Cal went on in a reassuring manner.

" I said I opposed hiring Jim. But while he was here, I backed him to the limit. He rubbed a lot of people the wrong way, but his big crime was that he didn't deliver. Had we won a championship, or even licked Rossiter a couple of times, the same men knocking him now would be slapping him on the back. That's human nature, Ed.

" Furthermore, Jim made it easier to hire you when the time came," Cal continued. " Since importing athletes didn't pay, it was obvious that we ought to return to our old aims — a representative team coached by a man who knew the Hastings traditions. And who better than a Hastings man like yourself, young and energetic, who has already proved he can teach the game? This is a big university, Ed, but we prefer our sports without high pressure, we've discovered. You're not expected to win 'em all."

" I'll remember that when we lose our first one," Savage said, to cover his embarrassment.

Murchison's blue eyes twinkled.

" You do that. And forget about Regan. In every big alumni group, there's someone who's agin the coach, or the president, or the school policy, or the color of the new buildings. That's Marty, a born 'aginner.' "

Maybe that wasn't quite an accurate description of Regan, Savage reflected, but the rest of it made sense. Cal had been quite frank with him, and unmistakably sincere.

It was going to be quite an adventure, come fall.

3

NOT like that, Larry, for the love of mud! You want to break his leg? "

Sam LaCosta's voice cracked like rifle fire, piercing the assorted noises of the practice field. Savage, fifty feet away, swiveled around in astonishment. Sam rarely raised his voice in such fashion.

LaCosta had planted himself in front of Larry Hearst, and was making a sawing motion with one hand. It was as though a bulldog was snarling at a great Dane, for the stocky coach had to tilt his head back to look into the face of the towering sophomore tackle.

Savage decided he had better inquire.

" Run that 41 series again, Kas," he told the quarterback who had been directing an eleven through signal drill. " Down to the fence and back."

Then he started toward the middle of the field, where LaCosta had been holding blocking drill with some of the linemen. It was late September; the opener against Warwick was only four days away.

Hearst, a curly-haired youngster with a ruddy complexion, was standing mute before LaCosta, looking abashed.

" What's up, Sam? "

"Somewhere this kid's picked up that whip-around leg block," LaCosta said, glowering. "I've been trying to explain that it can cripple a man."

Savage's gray eyes showed a flicker of concern. The whip-around took its name from the manner in which the blocker, after throwing himself in front of an opponent, followed through by "whipping" his legs around and behind the other man's. It was effective in that it generally knocked the man off his feet, but many coaches believed it caused leg or ankle injuries. Although there was nothing in the rule book to forbid it, these coaches would not teach the block. Savage guessed that Jim Trainor had not been one of that group. There had been other signs that some of the Hastings players knew a few tricks not in the manual — the quick jab with the heel of the hand, the elbow, the clenched fist — all difficult for an official to detect if used in close line play. It was precisely those tactics Savage had determined he would not tolerate.

"Sam's right, Larry, it's a dangerous piece of business," he said quietly. Aware that the other players were listening with avid interest, he turned toward them.

"Men, watch that whipcrack. We don't use it here. O.K., Sam, take 'em again."

Vince Crump, standing with arms folded across his chest, murmured something to his neighbor, Bob Clawson, the senior center. Clawson snickered. The sound stung Savage and his immediate reaction was anger. He would stop and ask Crump loudly if he could share in the joke.

But he did not. Things had been moving smoothly since the start of practice, at least on the surface, and he did not want to roil the waters without good reason.

Yet he could not rid himself of an uneasiness that he could not pinpoint. He was not by nature a disciplinarian, but he had resolved firmly that there would be no doubt

31

who was the boss. Marty Regan's words had cut deep.

And yet, a coach could not tell a squad in so many words that he expected them to give up dirty football. Instead, he had stressed the uselessness of such infractions as illegal use of the hands, holding, or piling on a runner.

"You might get away with it now and then," he had said. "But when you do get caught, it means fifteen yards, and it could mean the ball game too, if it cancels a long gain."

What impression that had made he did not really know. Habit was hard to break, he discovered. Some of the linemen instinctively brought their clenched fists up from their chests when they charged. LaCosta had groaned about that.

"If I had to play against that stuff consistently," he groused, "I'd slug somebody."

"They'll change, Sam. They'll change or get out."

So far, there had been no overt challenge to his authority. Even Crump had taken instructions with an impassive stolidity, and the other veterans imported by Jim Trainor had followed Vince's example.

Perhaps, Savage thought, the Scarsella incident had jarred Vince a little. The halfback, after undergoing an operation on his injured knee, had been advised by Dr. Beardsley to play no more football.

One other circumstance contributed to Savage's uncertainty. As Crump was unmistakably the bellwether of one group, so Junior Travis was the central figure of another, composed principally of players who had come to Hastings through channels not directed by Trainor. The two had little in common, and Trainor knew that factions could be potential dynamite on a football team.

It worried him as it did LaCosta, but he tried to be cheerful about it.

"Whether they pal around or not is none of our business," he reminded Sam. "Let 'em be standoffish with one another on the social level, if that's the way they want it. Wait until they start getting haughty on the field before we get nervous about it."

So he did not pick up Crump for his low-voiced aside. Not now, this close to the Cavaliers' first game.

As it approached, Savage was developing a fine case of buck fever. Winning the opener under a new coach could give the team a measure of confidence.

It would also give me some confidence, he reflected wryly. At this stage he was flying blind. By his own standards, he had perhaps half a dozen players who he was sure would be first stringers on most college teams. Crump, of course; Bob Clawson at center; Mike Mahoney at tackle; Al Glass at quarter; and Junior Travis at halfback. Larry Hearst was powerful but crude, but he was going to be a good one. There were others who had promise too, but it would take time, and coaching.

Still, the limited information on Warwick he could gather from the pictures of last year's game and the notes of George Breck did not portray the Panthers as a powerhouse. The Cavaliers had beaten them narrowly the year before, 19–14, but year in and year out, Warwick did not have the "horses" to be found at Rossiter and Linfield and Mount Royal. Nor did Hastings, Savage thought.

One thing the Cavaliers would have in their favor Saturday was the surprise element. Jim Trainor had been a split-T-formation man, but Savage knew he did not have the personnel for that attack. There were all too few power runners on his squad; the Cavaliers could not hope to run over any opponents. They would have to outcute them, substituting finesse for brute strength.

So Savage had decided that a combination of the

33

straight T formation with flankers and a few split-T series added was best suited to his material. It was nothing revolutionary; many teams combined the two. But each coach had his own small variations, and Warwick could only guess at Savage's.

As the coaches were dressing after the workout, George Breck asked, " Ed, will we scrimmage tomorrow? "

Breck was rangy, sandy-haired, and thin-faced, with a hawklike profile. Savage liked him, although he felt that George was instinctively comparing his own methods with those of Jim Trainor. That would be a natural reaction. Perhaps it would have been wiser to play the role of new broom and sweep away every vestige of the old regime, Savage thought, but the man he had wanted for Breck's post had not been available. And George had a reputation as an excellent assistant.

" I don't think so," Savage replied. " Some of the boys are sort of banged up."

" You think we've had enough? We've had only two — " Breck trailed off dubiously.

" I know, but we've done a lot of running and had a lot of individual contact work. Maybe we'll have a line scrimmage Thursday, but that's all. I'd like to come up to this first one healthy, George. We're awful thin in some spots."

" Yeah, I know." Breck's voice lacked conviction and Savage was a trifle annoyed. He knew that Trainor had held frequent scrimmages during the early days of practice. Savage would have liked to do so, too, but there had been an alarming crop of sore muscles, sprains, and bruises in the first week. At least three of the eleven he planned to start against Warwick would require enough tape and bandages to qualify at first sight as invalids.

Babe Bassich, the small frosh coach, combed his sparse hair over a bald spot and grumped: " Kids are flabby

34

these days, that's what. Too many automobiles."

"I know you're not, Babe," Savage said with a chuckle. Babe had been a great broken-field runner in college, and now, twenty-five years later, he was still hard-muscled. "I only wish you were playing safety for us Saturday."

"Me? I'd need a net to catch a punt," Bassich said, but he was obviously pleased.

"I'm not sure Glass doesn't need one." Savage sounded perplexed. "I can't figure Al on that. He does everything else well, but he seems to come apart when he sees that ball up in the sky. And yet I don't want to play him at halfback on defense where he'd have to make more tackles and maybe get racked up."

"Al's never played safety before," Breck put in. "He's uncertain back there. He told me it makes him nervous."

Savage's eyebrows went up.

"He says that, does he?" he murmured. "Well, if it's going to unhinge him, maybe we'll change."

He concealed his displeasure. He'd worked hard with the quarterback on punt returns and Glass had tried diligently to master the comparatively simple stunt. But he had never mentioned nervousness to Savage. Instead he had confided in an assistant coach.

LaCosta, who had been silent, asked suddenly: "Babe, where would Hearst pick up that whip-around block? Not from you, I suppose?"

"I should say not!" Bassich erupted indignantly. "I've seen too many kids hurt to teach that one!"

"Oh, it's not that bad, Babe," Breck said soothingly. "You know it's used. Larry's just a kid; I suppose he saw someone do it and tried to imitate him."

Savage felt it time to intervene.

"Larry won't try it again; Sam gave him the word to-day. No point in banging it around. Remember, we look at the Warwick pictures again tonight — seven-thirty."

Afterward, he said to Sam: " You sure put Babe through the roof with that question. Didn't you know he'd resent it? "

" I wanted to know if I had to unlearn any more frosh," LaCosta said with a trace of surliness. " You don't get answers if you don't ask questions."

Savage let it drop. He guessed that Sam, like himself, was getting a little jumpy before the first game.

Jake Gledhill's portly figure was waiting for Savage at the gate to the practice field after Thursday's session, and he joined him on the walk to the gym.

" 'Just before the battle, Mother,' " he remarked. " What've you got here, Ed? "

Savage was about to reply that he couldn't tell whether Hastings was going to win by six touchdowns or lose by ten, which was only a slightly exaggerated reflection of his own state of mind. But he knew that the players, all of them avid followers of the sports pages, would not be cheered by such a statement. Why should they display self-confidence if the coach didn't?

" Jake," Savage said with a heartiness he did not feel, " I think we're going to win Saturday. We can beat Warwick."

Gledhill stopped and pushed his spectacles up to his forehead.

" Well, that's a refreshing outlook. You're not talking off the record? I can quote you as predicting a win? "

" Sure," Savage answered, already wishing he hadn't predicted anything except that Hastings would show up for the game. But he couldn't weasel on Gledhill now. " Sure. Understand, I'm not belittling Warwick. But I think we've got the makings of a fair team, and we'll get better as we go along."

Jake pulled his glasses down to their proper niche and made notes on a folded wad of paper.

"Pretty good team, will get better," he mumbled as he scribbled, then looked up owlishly. "Anyone on the schedule you don't think Hastings can beat?"

"Now wait a minute, Jake," Savage said in alarm. "We have to play 'em one at a time. Don't paint me into a corner."

"O.K., I'll rephrase it. Which teams do you think you can't beat?"

"Take it easy!" Savage said despairingly. "All I meant to say was that we weren't conceding any games before the season started. I'm not claiming we'll win 'em all."

"Sure, I understand that," the sports writer said. "Don't worry, Ed, I'm not trying to make you look foolish. But it's a switch when a coach doesn't go into mourning about his team's chances. Unless, of course, you'd rather I just forgot everything you've said and we started over."

Savage grinned crookedly. Jake had him boxed, and knew it.

"Of course not. That's what I said. Print it if you like."

When he read it next morning in the *Tribune,* Savage was not sorry. Gledhill had been as good as his word. The Hastings coach did not sound brash or cocky, but he had most certainly forecast a win over Warwick.

"Ed Savage is not selling his boys short, no matter whom they play," Gledhill's column concluded. "I approve of that attitude."

Savage hoped the players did too. So did Sam LaCosta.

"That's the stuff to feed the troops, Ed. Let 'em know *you* think they're good, even if they aren't."

To his astonishment, the column ruffled Murchison, who telephoned him in midmorning.

"Didn't you get your neck out a little far, Ed?" he inquired somewhat crossly. " Sounds to me like a ready-made fight talk for Warwick."

Somewhat taken aback, Savage explained that he wanted his team to go in thinking it could win, that he thought it would help their morale if the coach was on record that they could.

" I don't put much stock in fight talks, Cal," he said defensively. " Kids these days are much too sophisticated to be stirred up by that kind of emotional appeal. When it comes to mental attitude, I believe a team gets itself ready for a game. I don't think we'll be flat for this one."

He saw himself exhorting Crump and Clawson and Whitney to fight hard for the glory of the old school and grimaced. He'd be blown out of the dressing room on a gale of laughter.

" I hope for your sake they're not flat," Murchison said, sounding unconvinced. " I wouldn't want you to get off on the wrong foot, Ed."

Why didn't I keep my big trap shut? Savage wondered moodily after Cal hung up. It would have been just as easy to tell Gledhill he was scared to death of the Panthers.

He had further reason to doubt the wisdom of his forecast that afternoon when the Panthers flew in. As a matter of courtesy, Savage drove to the airport to greet them and their coach, Fred Berry, whom he had never met.

Berry, a florid-faced Oklahoman, grinned affably as he shook hands.

" Kinda leery of playing yore team tewmorra," he drawled. " Read where you plan to whup us good."

Some of the Warwick players — a husky lot too, Savage noted gloomily — were standing behind their coach and he heard a few derisive snorts.

"Not planning, just hoping," Savage parried. "And not whupping, either, just winning. One point would suit me fine."

"Likewise," Berry conceded genially. "Hope we get a crowd. You know the old saying — 'It matters not whether you won or lost, but how many paid to see the game.'"

"I think there are tickets still available," Savage answered dryly.

Sarah Fleming called him Saturday morning.

"I hope I didn't wake you up, Ed. I know it's only eight thirty, but I have a nine o'clock class and I did want to wish you luck. How do you feel?"

"Never felt better in my life, doll. But of course, I've had a miserable life."

"Lunatic. I did wake you, didn't I?"

"Are you kidding? I'm on my sixth cup of coffee. Do you think I slept a wink last night?"

"Oh, dear," she sighed. "I suppose you didn't, at that. Seems so silly."

"Only a game, I know." He was faintly ironic. "But I hope you're going to see it. Need tickets?"

"Yes, I shall, and no, I don't, thank you. Faculty section, 45-yard line, row 51."

"I forgot about that piece of faculty gravy."

"Don't get flip with me, young man," Sarah said primly. "Remember, I have three of your beasts in my English comp. class, and if they can't tackle any better than they write, heaven help Hastings."

"Jupiter, now I have to be nice to English teachers," he groaned. "And some people think coaching is easy."

She laughed delightedly.

"Any time you wish to be nice, call me. Now go out and win, hero. I'll be rooting hard."

He felt better after that. In truth, he had slept badly. Was he being smart in planning a wide six defense? What information he had, indicated Warwick had no good long passer. If it was wrong, the Cavaliers might get killed in the first few minutes.

And what about Olvera at fullback, instead of Freeman? He knew Olvera was too slow to make the toss-outs go, but Freeman was a high-strung youngster with a tendency to fumble. Loss of the ball early on a bobble could be a terrific psychological blow.

The longer he lay awake, the more hopeless Hastings' cause appeared. In his tortured mind, all the Panthers were ten feet tall, with three arms.

In the light of day, he knew it wasn't that bad.

Sam LaCosta emerged from the other bedroom, yawning and scratching himself aimlessly.

" Well, today the balloon goes up, eh, Ed? "

" That's a nice way to put it. Maybe I'll go up with it. Truly, I don't remember being this jittery before games at Niles. Were you? "

LaCosta's black eyes came alive and he whacked Savage on the back.

" Come on, boy, don't die in the dressing room. I thought you were full of the old confeedence. Were you kidding Gledhill? "

" Not exactly. Only, well — "

" Ah-r-r. We've got a good team, man, a *good* team. That's what I read somewhere, anyway. We'll breeze."

" You're such a help, Sambo," Savage said wanly.

What did help, however, was the complete lack of any signs of nervousness on the part of the veterans when the squad gathered in the dressing room. Crump and Whitney joked loudly across the room; Clawson shied a helmet at Mahoney after some playful exchange, and Al Glass engaged in an impromptu wrestling match with Dave Rolph, the gray-haired trainer, until Savage told them sharply to knock it off.

"You're supposed to get 'em in shape, not twist 'em out of it, Dave," he said. The trainer, who had been clucking over Hastings players, Savage included, for fifteen years, merely grinned and resumed the taping of Glass's ankle.

But Junior Travis, quick to dress, was obviously fidgety. He examined his cleats, retied his laces, adjusted his hip pads, and made numerous trips to the drinking fountain.

Savage laid a hand on Junior's shoulder, and the halfback gave a perceptible start.

"Easy, Junior. You'll wear yourself out with all that stall-walking. I'm counting on you for yards today."

"I'm O.K.," Travis said shortly. He was a well-built 170-pounder with handsome, regular features and curly brown hair. There was a wariness about his attitude that disturbed Savage. The halfback seemed to be keeping him at arm's length, as though he did not trust the coach fully. Savage did not know why.

"Sure, you're O.K.," he told him. "But stay off your feet until we go."

And suddenly the time to go was on them, and Savage made a little speech, much like the ones he had made at Niles. Low-keyed and relaxed.

"I've said I think we'll win today," he concluded. "Please don't make a liar out of your coach."

There were a few laughs and they went out. The Panthers, in their light-blue jerseys, were already on the field, and the Cavaliers, wearing white with red arm bands and numbers, seemed much smaller than their opponents. It was a sunny day, but not hot enough to be oppressive, and Savage, scanning the stands in the sixty-thousand-seat stadium, was pleasantly surprised to find them already a

41

third full, an hour before game time.

Savage had appointed Crump game captain. He felt he could do no less. Vince was a senior and a natural leader. He had instructions to receive the kickoff if Hastings won the toss. It did.

"O.K., Al." Savage gripped Glass's arm as the quarterback jogged up and down. "Run Travis on the 57 first play, then it's up to you. You're the man in charge. And Al — let the punts roll. Don't try to field any on the fly. Got it?"

Glass looked startled, then sheepish, then relieved. Savage was not going to have the quarterback worrying about dropping punts, along with his other responsibilities. He only wished Al had told him about his uncertainty, rather than George Breck.

Then they were lining up, a whistle blew, and a figure in light blue moved forward toward the ball, teed up on the Warwick 40-yard line.

Ed Savage clenched his fingers into his moist palms and took a deep, deep breath.

4

THE ball was kicked low, bounding erratically down toward the left-hand corner. Savage gulped as it struck Travis on the chest and bounced off. Junior recovered it quickly, but the momentary bobble delayed the return just enough to permit a Panther to break through the blocking screen and pin Travis on the 18-yard line.

Savage sat down on the bench, although he did not stay there long. George Breck was seated at a small table to his right, a telephone headset clamped to his head. Sam LaCosta was on the other end of the line, high in the press box. Savage had found him a superb " spotter," quick to see the strong and weak points of patterns and tactics. A man standing at ground level near mid-field could not see details of the play unless it took place almost directly in front of him.

The Cavaliers came out in their flanker T. Tony Corbett, the right half, and Sid Maderas, the right end, were split wide, with Glass under the center, Travis and Olvera an arm's length apart behind him.

Without power runners, Savage had done what he could to compensate — forcing the defense to spread to meet the passing threat posed by the double flankers. Travis was a jolting runner and Glass a clever stepper as well as a finer passer, but that about summed it up at the moment. For a while, at least, the Hastings attack was going to be hit or miss.

"Ah-h-h!" He was on his feet eagerly as Glass handed off to Travis, who piled in over Warwick's left guard behind the forward charge of Crump and Hearst, playing shoulder to shoulder. The hole was there, and Junior's churning legs carried him past the 30 for a first down.

"That's our bread-and-butter play for sure," he exclaimed delightedly to Breck. Travis carrying, Crump and Hearst clearing the way. If Hastings ever got close to the foe's goal line, Savage had decided, that would be the play to take it over, every time.

His exultation gave way abruptly to chagrin and indignation. The referee had beckoned the Warwick captain to him, and was talking to him near the 20-yard line. That could only mean a penalty against the Cavaliers, and in a moment the official was trotting briskly down to the 7, then holding aloft his hands, his right hand grasping his left wrist. That was the signal for offensive holding — fifteen yards.

"Oh, for the love of —" Savage muttered in disappointment. "Let me have that phone, George. Hey, Sam, who was it?"

LaCosta's voice echoed his disgust.

"Whitney. Regular cobra clutch on the halfback."

Savage shook his head in frustration. He'd have a word with Mr. Whitney.

But that was routed from his mind at once, for Glass was faking a hand-off to Olvera, then circling to his right, the ball imperfectly concealed behind his right thigh.

"Oh, no!" Savage groaned in consternation. The Panther end clutched at Glass, five yards behind his own goal line, but Al wriggled away, leaped high, and threw.

44

At the Hastings 45-yard line, Tony Corbett had to turn and stop to make the catch. That gave the outmaneuvered Warwick safety a chance to overhaul him ten yards farther downfield as the Cavalier rooters yelled joyously.

There was a bewildered look on Savage's face. He had his doubts that the long pass from the end zone was the play to call in that situation, but Glass had made it work. Well, he had told Al to take charge.

From the Panther 45, Glass, waggling the ball in front of him as though he were pushing a baby carriage, slipped off tackle on a keeper play for eight. Olvera, heavy feet and all, banged for the first down on the 26 through a hole at center that looked so huge he might have walked through it on his hands.

Savage didn't need LaCosta's call then to tell him that someone was mopping up the Warwick middle.

"We can run there all day," Sam cackled happily. "Their line backers are 'way out in left field and those guards look as though they're made of cardboard."

"I think Glass has seen it, the way he's calling it. But they're bound to jam the center now."

Warwick did exactly that, and Glass sent Travis through the guard-tackle hole anyway for ten more. Savage caught a glimpse of a broad back wearing a red number 66 oblit- erating a Panther in the secondary. That would be Crump.

Then Olvera bobbled a toss-out from Glass on the option play and Savage buried his face in his hands for a mo- ment, sure the Cavaliers were going to blow it. Olvera recovered for two lost, but Glass simply gave it to Travis off the guard again, and Junior, seeing daylight, swerved to his right, put on a burst of speed, and went over in the right-hand corner.

As the noise from bench and stands hammered in his ears, Savage felt a little limp. He looked at the scoreboard clock. The Hastings touchdown had required little more than four minutes. It had seemed like forty.

Whitney, a deadly accurate place kicker in practice, sent this attempt skittering off to the right of the goal posts. Savage was filled with anxiety. He could already envision the Cavaliers losing, 7–6, all because Whit hurried his kick or Glass failed to set the ball down properly or something trivial.

As it developed, Savage might have saved himself that bit of self-torment. After Whitney had kicked off far past the goal line and the end zone too, Warwick started from the 20. On the second play, Larry Hearst shot through the line and hit the fullback head on. The ball popped out of the grasp of the badly jarred Panther, and Maderas coiled around it on the 15.

Glass immediately threw to Whitney on the goal line, a high riflelike pass which the big end caught over his head, before he tumbled into the end zone.

"Great steaming gumbo," Savage said in wonderment. Nothing like this had ever happened to him at Niles. Whitney kicked off again. Warwick made four yards in three tries and punted. From the Hastings 35, the Cavaliers scored again in six plays, Olvera going over from the 12 on a fullback draw play as Glass cleverly faked the pass.

That was enough to convince Savage the Cavaliers weren't going to lose the game, and he withdrew the entire first team. But the second eleven, with a squeaky-voiced soph quarterback named Kassowitz at the controls, pushed over another score while keeping the inept Panthers from crossing mid-field, and at half time Hastings had a 27–0 lead.

LaCosta came bubbling into the dressing room grinning like a catfish.

"You don't need anyone in the press box, Ed, so I think

46

I'll go home," he exulted. "We haven't done anything wrong so far. When's the last time you had a four-touchdown lead at half? Or you, George?"

"I don't believe we ever scored four touchdowns in one game at Niles, did we?" Savage inquired, as though it were not real. "I never dreamed Warwick would be so weak. Did you, George?"

Breck, too, seemed astounded at the Cavaliers' superiority.

"I suppose those two quick sixes unbuttoned 'em, but even so, they look horrible. I've never seen such sloppy tackling. And disorganized? They act as though they met one another for the first time just outside the stadium today."

"Well," said Savage with a whimsical expression, "this poses a problem I've never encountered before. How do we keep the score down? I'd like to get a longer look at the first string, but the way they're going, it could be 100."

"Oh, put 'em back in for a while," Breck advised. "They need the work, and they barely got warmed up."

Savage agreed with that, but he certainly did not want to pour it on a helpless opponent.

"I think I'll start the seconds," he declared. "They can use the game experience."

But the seconds, with the fleet Jack Freeman breaking for two long runs from the fullback spot, scored again in the first eight minutes of the third period, and gave every evidence of ability to repeat.

So Savage got them out of there and sent in what was left. There were forty-five men suited up on the Hastings bench, but eight or ten of them were football players only because they were dressed that way. Such was Savage's private opinion, and he had not anticipated getting down that far — certainly not in the opening game.

47

After that, the contest took on the aspects of a sand-lot affair, with numerous fumbles and penalties for off side. The Panthers even presented Hastings with still another touchdown by bobbling a punt, and kicked away two scoring chances of their own through misplays.

Savage kept looking at the clock, hoping that the sloppy performance would end. He was almost unhappy when, at the end, the Panthers reached the Cavalier 10-yard line and failed to score because a string-bean Hastings end named Murphy smothered the passer on fourth down. Savage was genuinely sorry Warwick had not made the touchdown to ease its humiliation just a little. But it was 41–0 at the gun, and as he crossed the field to shake hands with Berry, Savage's jubilance was diluted by sympathy for the loser.

" I'm sorry it went that high, Fred," he said with a note of apology. " We were shot full of luck all the way."

Berry took the proffered hand briefly. He looked sick.

" Thanks," he muttered and walked away, shoulders drooping. He was facing a long, dismal season and he knew it.

But how long could a coach be depressed by a 41–0 victory? Savage walked on air into the noisy enthusiasm of the Cavalier dressing room and made the rounds, scattering compliments among the happy crew. Even Junior Travis seemed to unbend a little.

" Aw, anyone could have run through those holes," he responded to Savage's words of praise. " I didn't have to do very much."

Vince Crump was being helped out of his jersey by Clawson.

" Nice game, Vince. You too, Bob. You chewed 'em up good."

" Game? That was no game, Coach," Crump said in a

48

loud voice. " That wasn't even a good scrimmage. I don't even need a shower."

"Well, take one anyway, just for the sake of appearances," Savage said jocularly. Crump's manner never failed to annoy him, and he suspected Vince knew it. But a guard of Crump's caliber might be given a little leeway.

But not too much, he promised himself grimly, as he headed for a small room across the corridor, where the sports writers awaited him.

When Savage awoke next morning, he lay for several minutes merely gazing contentedly at the ceiling and luxuriating in his status as a successful coach. For a week, anyway.

Only one minor incident had marred the day. Among the writers who had talked to him after the game were two who had accompanied the Panthers on the trip. One had asked Savage, in a rather unpleasant tone, if he had tried to run up the score to make an impression in his first game.

Choking back the indignant reply that rose to his lips, Savage had answered with careful politeness, pointing out that the Hastings starters had played only ten minutes, and the second team not much longer than that.

"We're not that much better than Warwick," he continued, aware that he was putting truth to a great strain. "We got some big breaks early, that's all."

The Warwick writer did not lose his look of bitter skepticism.

"I suppose he'll clobber me for shutting the gates of mercy," Savage said morosely to Sam LaCosta. Sam observed that there were sorehead sports writers and partisan sports writers, and this one appeared to be both, and that

Savage had better get used to the type.

At the other end of the scale, he had been overwhelmed by alumni enthusiasm, particularly that displayed by Murchison.

"It was terrific, Ed, terrific," Cal kept repeating, beaming. "I don't think we've ever won an opener that big — not since I've been around. I'll bet the Board members are happy enough now."

"Don't let 'em get too happy, Cal," Savage cautioned. "We simply aren't that good. Naturally, I can't say out loud that Warwick was just plain awful, but that's what it amounted to."

Murchison's high spirits could not be deflated so easily, and Savage did not persist. Time would do that, he thought wryly. In fact, next Saturday might do it.

Next Saturday, the Cavaliers must go south to meet Linfield, and the Braves would be quite a different cup of tea from the Panthers. Savage would not know the details until Babe Bassich returned on the noon plane from his scouting assignment on the Braves. Yesterday he had seen them defeat a good Texas eleven; last year they had defeated Hastings by two touchdowns.

Meanwhile, Savage knew he had plenty of chores at home. He had to work some more with Glass on punts; there was no reason why the quarterback, who lacked neither nerve nor dexterity, should quail at catching a ball. Hearst was going to be a fine tackle, but he charged in straight like a blind bull. A good team would trap him. Whitney was in for a lecture on his tendency to hold. And then there were the reserves who had looked promising — Kassowitz at quarter; Bedolla, one of Marty Regan's boys, at end; and Fitzgerald, a chubby, freckle-faced sophomore guard. Sonny Casper, the other first-string guard, was not too strong, although Savage admitted that it might be because he suffered by comparison with Crump. If anything happened to Vince . . .

Bassich's report on Linfield was voluminous and not encouraging. The Braves had started six of the eleven who had opened against Hastings last year, including an All-American halfback, Haggerty. They were a split-T team, strong line, not much passing.

"Morris, the quarterback, runs the keeper pretty well," Bassich advised, poring over his notebook. "Number 36 — that's Devoe — runs the fullback counter O.K., but he's kind of slow. Haggerty is the one to watch, of course, but they've got a soph named Rose at the other halfback who's just as fast, but not as smart. If either of 'em gets to the outside, look out! "

It was eight o'clock in the evening before the coaches finished rerunning the pictures of last year's game. When the lights were turned on, Savage looked at the statistics, which he had only glanced at before, and a figure jumped at him.

"Jupiter! I missed this. We lost a hundred and twenty-five yards in penalties and they lost a hundred! What went on, George? "

Breck rubbed his nose.

"It was a rugged game, Ed," he said with a significant look. "Both teams were laying the wood for fair."

One of those, Savage thought. Plenty of calls for unnecessary roughness, he surmised.

Aloud, he said: "I hope we're rugged, but if we lose anything like a hundred and twenty-five yards on penalties, there'll be some changes made. That's ridiculous! "

It was a lot, Breck conceded, but added, "Those Braves weren't just making mud pies out there."

Savage decided he'd like to know a little more about that game from someone with a detached point of view.

Next day he called Jake Gledhill.

"This is a question in confidence, Jake. Last year's Linfield game — was it unusually rough?"

Gledhill gave a dry chuckle.

"I wouldn't call it *unusually* rough, because no one got killed. There was one fist fight, I remember, and afterward in the dressing room Len Waterman, the Linfield coach, said he didn't want to play Hastings again, ever. Two or three of his boys got hurt.

"Of course, a coach can't go spouting off that he won't play another school in the Conference. Len would never have said it if he hadn't been real hot. So when he got back home, they put the pressure on him and made him back up. He had to claim he hadn't said that at all, but was misquoted. Except he said it, all right. I was there."

"Oh, swell," Savage said glumly. "They must be waiting for us down there."

"I wouldn't be surprised. I hope it doesn't discourage you from making another fearless prediction of victory for Hastings."

"See me later in the week. And thanks, Jake."

Savage hung up and sat staring unhappily at the phone. He had the job of reaping the whirlwind Jim Trainor had sown.

5

THE Cavaliers flew down to Linfield on Friday afternoon in a chartered plane. It was only a two-hour flight, and Savage planned a brief workout in the Braves' stadium after their arrival.

Some of the players read, others dozed. Among the dozers was Jake Gledhill, who hadn't missed a Hastings game, at home or away, for several years.

Savage, seated near the back of the plane, was going over Bassich's scout report for perhaps the twentieth time when Cal Murchison sat down beside him.

"Think we can win this one, Ed?"

"We *can*, but we'll have to be awful lucky. They're a pretty sound team, Cal, and frankly, we're not. And I imagine Waterman will have them revved up for us after last year."

Murchison's forehead furrowed for a moment.

"Oh, that. It wasn't nearly as bad as Len made out. Besides," he lowered his voice, "he was sore at Trainor. He's got nothing against you."

Savage said he appreciated that, but there remained the tactical problem of containing Haggerty and Rose, among others.

"Well, I hope we get over them," Murchison said, rising.

" It could mean the start of a big season for us, really big."

He made his way down the aisle, leaving Savage a bit perplexed. He hadn't expected Cal to count on a win tomorrow, but he had been given that distinct impression.

The Linfield athletic director, a gaunt, gray-haired man named Patrick, met the Cavaliers at the airport, but the coach, Waterman, was not in evidence. Patrick acknowledged the introductions to Savage and LaCosta cordially enough, but his exchange with Murchison was short and businesslike, with nothing of personal warmth. He drove off by himself as the Cavaliers boarded the special bus waiting to take them to their hotel.

"Was it my imagination or did I detect a slight chill?" LaCosta asked in a low voice. "That joker didn't seem even a little bit glad to see us."

"I've had heartier welcomes," Savage conceded uneasily.

As the players trooped into the hotel lobby, some went to the newsstand and bought copies of the local papers. Savage heard Mike Mahoney give a whoop.

"Listen to this, will you?" he exclaimed gleefully. "'Memories of last year's blood bath at Hastings will be uppermost in the minds of Linfield's Braves tomorrow when they play host to the Cavaliers before a crowd forecast at fifty thousand.'"

He looked around with an innocent air.

"Blood bath! I don't remember any blood, do you, Vince?"

"Just my own," Crump said with a one-sided grin. "As I recall, someone stepped on my face. In fun, of course."

Savage moved swiftly across the lobby.

"May I see that paper, Mike?" he asked quietly. The big tackle handed it to him with an amused look, and

54

Savage read the story hurriedly, indignation rising in him with every paragraph.

But he masked his feelings as he handed the paper back to Mahoney.

"I wish the guy who wrote that had to play tomorrow," he said, forcing a smile. Then he raised his voice. "All right, fellows, get your rooms and then come right downstairs. We leave for the stadium in twenty minutes."

"What else did the story say, Ed?" LaCosta asked in the privacy of their room.

"There was a lot more like it," Savage rasped. "You'd think we came down here with brass knuckles on every man."

"Suppose it gets sticky tomorrow?"

"Sam, there's going to be no rough stuff on our part," Savage said grimly. "I intend to make that clear to everybody. If I have to lose every game, I'm going to clean up Hastings football. Cal Murchison's behind me on that, I'm sure."

"Good boy," LaCosta said brusquely. "I don't want to be in on any brawls, either."

Certainly the newspaper article had not intimidated many of the Cavaliers. As they limbered up in sweat suits at the stadium, Savage saw Bob Clawson going through an exaggerated shadow-boxing routine.

"Just getting in shape for the game," the center explained to Whitney, swinging a mighty right at an imaginary foe. There was a burst of laughter at this. Savage did not join in. He would have a few words on the subject.

He spoke to them the next afternoon, just before the Cavaliers went out on the field.

"There's been a good deal of nonsense in the papers here about this game," he began. "I imagine all of you have read it. Well, forget it. We're here to play football, nothing else. I don't care what Linfield does, the first man I see pull anything out of line comes out and stays out.

"Travis, you're the game captain. If you see something that isn't being called, tell the referee. Don't beef to him and don't whine. Just tell him about it. Any questions?"

In the silence that followed, Savage could hear the men breathing. Travis was obviously surprised by his selection as captain. Savage had made the choice because he believed Junior to be a cool head who would not hesitate to crack down on his own men if necessary.

Crump was the first to speak.

"Aren't we allowed to protect ourselves if they start cutting up, Coach? Or do we just turn the other cheek?"

Savage's eyes narrowed at the gibe.

"There are four officials out there to protect you, Vince," he said evenly. "What I said goes — for everybody. Any more questions?"

Again silence.

"Fine," Savage said with a cheerfulness he did not feel. "Now let's go out and lick 'em."

As the coaches followed the team out of the tunnel onto the sun-splashed green turf, Savage heard a noise like the pounding of waves on a beach. It took him a moment to comprehend that it was concerted booing from the Linfield rooting section on the far side of the stadium, and that it was meant for the Cavaliers.

He turned toward Breck, appalled. "I've never heard anything like that before!"

"It is a rowdy bunch," George said uneasily. "Usually they don't start so early, though. Frankly, Ed, I think the boys ought to know they're not wearing handcuffs if it gets stormy."

Troubled creases showed around Savage's eyes.

"George, I'm hoping we've been borrowing trouble. Waterman wants to win this game too, and he knows you can't play good football if you're only thinking about getting the other fellow. I think Linfield will stick to football, in spite of that rooting section. And so will we."

Breck did not reply, but it was obvious that he did not approve.

A tremendous cheer went up as the Linfield squad streamed onto the field, followed by scattered jeers as the stripe-shirted officials made their appearance.

The referee, Bill Ogden, had worked games in which Savage had played, and Ed knew him as one who did not fear the crowd. He did not know the others, and he could only hope that they were not "homers" — officials who hesitated to make adverse decisions against the home team.

Ogden came over to shake hands with Savage.

"I see we've all got friends here," Ed commented. Ogden laughed and said he didn't mind so long as they weren't armed.

"Let's have a nice clean game, Ed," he added.

"Let's," Savage agreed, wooden-faced. They understood each other. Ogden had read the local papers too.

Whitney kicked off for the Cavaliers, a long one into the end zone, and against a background of incessant noise Linfield started from the 20.

Savage's stomach settled back into its normal position. He felt that Hastings would be able to score on the Braves, whose pass defense had been spotty last week. The question was whether the defense he had set up — to keep the Linfield halfbacks from getting outside the ends — could hold the Braves to one or two touchdowns. To contain Haggerty and Rose, he was prepared to give Linfield the short gains up the middle. It was up to Crump and Clawson, the outside line backers, to turn the wide plays to the inside.

Not unexpectedly, the Braves sent Haggerty on a sweep at left end as their first effort. Sid Maderas drifted with the runner and Clawson came up to nail Haggerty with only two yards gained.

The same play with Rose carrying to the other side gained another two as Tony Corbett ran him out of bounds.

So far, so good, Savage thought, then winced as Morris, the quarterback, simply took the ball from center and plowed straight ahead for the first down.

In the ensuing four minutes Savage realized, with a sinking feeling, that his hopes had exceeded his reason. The Braves moved thirty yards in seven plays, all but one inside the tackles. Finding the outside lanes clogged, Morris switched to the simple split-T power shots, the dive-tackle play, and the cross bucks. Haggerty could not only sprint in the open, he could also drive, and the Cavaliers could not hold him to less than four yards.

Savage had anticipated the move, but he had hoped that the Cavalier line would meet the challenge in better style. At least to the point of spoiling one play in each sequence of downs and putting Linfield in a hole.

"Sam says they're hammering at Casper," Breck reported glumly. "They're getting the jump on us up front."

"Looks like they've got the horses, all right," Savage agreed. Clymer, the Braves' big left guard, was just too much for Casper to handle.

Linfield came up to the ball on the run, like a team that knew it was rolling. From the Hastings 38, Morris swung to his right on the option play. Mahoney fought off a blocker and grabbed for the quarterback, but Morris got the pitchout away just in time to Haggerty, darting wide.

Savage sucked in his breath. Maderas had been cut down; Clawson was blocked by two white-shirted Braves. Corbett wheeled up fast from defensive halfback — too fast, for Haggerty, with a neat change of pace, fooled him badly. He was outside and straightening for the run down the side line when a bright red jersey flashed seemingly from nowhere.

It was Crump, who had trailed the play from the other side. Haggerty, concentrating on eluding Corbett and looking downfield, had no warning. Crump hit him in the small of the back with a terrific jolt.

The two went down in front of the Hastings bench, not five yards from Savage, who breathed again in relief as Vince arose. He had not seen Crump, either. The man was a football player, no doubt of that.

Then he saw that Haggerty still lay face down on the turf, motionless. Instinctively, he took a step toward the stricken youth before he remembered that a coach needed the referee's permission to go on the playing field. But a trainer did not, and Dave Rolph was already scurrying to the spot.

" Man, was he hit! " Breck said feelingly.

The Linfield trainer and team doctor had now reached the prostrate player, and in a moment he was stirring feebly. Dave Rolph returned to the bench.

" Knocked cold, that's all," he said with professional detachment. " Doesn't know where he is or what day it is."

" Thank goodness," Savage said fervently. Haggerty was helped up and led unsteadily from the field to the sound of sympathetic hand clapping.

Then abruptly there came an ominous chant from the Linfield rooting section. It took Savage a moment to understand it. When he did, he went pale with anger.

" Get that dirty 66, get that dirty 66."

59

He whirled toward Breck.

"Those maniacs!" he burst out fiercely. "That was a good, hard tackle — there was nothing dirty about it. You saw it!"

"Sure it was," Breck assented, but he looked worried. "But the whole blasted school has been keyed up for us, and they're just itching for a chance to talk ugly. Makes no difference how the kid got hurt."

Across the field, the Linfield yell-leaders were trying to quiet the rooters with little success. Finally Waterman turned and held up his arms for silence. The chant died away slowly to a low rumble, like some underground disturbance that might erupt again without warning.

During the time out, the red-shirted Cavaliers had clustered near the 30-yard line. Crump was smiling as he looked toward the bench, giving no sign that he had paid attention to the Linfield stands.

For a moment, Savage considered taking Vince out of the game. If the Braves were going to lay for him, Crump deserved protection. But taking him out would not only weaken Hastings immeasurably, it could be interpreted as an admission that Haggerty had been a victim of dirty play.

He decided to let Vince remain. On the next play, Morris mishandled the snapback from center and fell on it for another loss. On fourth down, Rose, cutting back over tackle, was two yards short of the needed distance, and for the first time that day Savage felt as though he could smile.

The Cavaliers had used only a few plays in beating Warwick, and Savage had pinned some reliance on those the Linfield scouts had not seen because they had not been needed.

Glass, sensing that the Braves might be somewhat unsettled after losing their best runner and the ball too, decided the moment was opportune to take his surprise shots. He called a quick jump pass to Maderas, who broke sharply to the middle from his position on the flank. Maderas was cutting through the secondary almost before the startled Braves knew the play was under way. The safety ran him out of bounds five yards past mid-field.

" Screen pass, Al, screen pass," Savage whispered prayerfully. Glass sent Freeman into the middle instead, and he got only a yard, but he had the screener up his sleeve. He raced straight back from the center, his eyes roving downfield as Linfield linemen poured through on him.

At the last possible moment, he turned left and tossed a little lob over the heads of two charging Braves to Travis, who had delayed, then sneaked out to the side. There were four Cavaliers in front of him as he caught. They mowed a path for him for ten yards, and then Junior broke clear of Rose's desperate diving tackle and fled to the end zone untouched.

" Well! he made it! " Savage said in wonderment as the Cavalier bench exploded in back-pounding delight. He was too surprised to yell. He had counted on that screen pass to work the first time the Cavaliers uncovered it, but hardly that well. Not until Whitney kicked the seventh point out of Glass's hold did he grasp exactly what it represented. Hastings was in front of its favored foe.

Shortly thereafter he was screaming as loudly as his voice would permit, for the Cavaliers had scored again.

The quick touchdown had given Hastings a tremendous lift, and Haggerty's loss took the keen edge off Linfield's attack. The Braves did not make the first down following the kickoff, and Morris dropped back to kick.

Hearst went in like a rocket. He smashed past one defender and then leaped high in the air over the crouching figure of the blocker nearest Morris as the latter swung his foot.

The ball struck Larry's upraised hand with a loud "splat," and bounded crazily back toward the Linfield goal. Morris turned to chase it, but Maderas was already past him. Sid did not fall on the ball; instead, he scooped it up on the run, a maneuver for which Savage would have cheerfully shot him had he attempted it in practice. Maderas was in the end zone before Ed had time to think about it, and across the way Len Waterman crumpled his hat in his hands and dashed it to the turf.

Breck pounded his fist ecstatically on the telephone table and made unintelligible noises for a while, then demanded breathlessly: "You see Larry climb over that guy? The kid's an All-American right now!"

Savage was of no mind to debate it. The Cavaliers had drilled on punt-blocking patterns, of course, but this hadn't been one of them. Hearst had accomplished it on his own fierce charge.

Whitney kicked the extra to make it 14–0. The Linfield left end, smashing in viciously, hurled himself through the air in an attempt to block the boot and crash squarely into Glass, still on one knee after setting up the ball.

It could have been accidental. Glass got up slowly, put both hands to his face, then collapsed. Vince Crump, his face twisted in an ugly snarl, hooked one hand inside the Linfield end's shoulder pad and jerked him to his feet. Instantly, there was a swarm of red and white jerseys around the pair.

Here we go, Savage thought. But Ogden and another official leaped into the middle of the group, and in a moment the referee emerged holding the still angry Crump by one elbow, while the other official firmly guided the Linfield end in the other direction.

Glass was on his feet again, shaking his head as though to clear it. Clawson had one arm around the quarterback's shoulders as Dave Rolph ran out to him.

Concerned though he was about Glass, Savage felt a vast relief when he perceived that Crump was not being ejected. Ogden had turned back toward the Linfield goal and now Junior Travis was talking to the big guard, who was making wrathful gestures.

"Kassowitz! Fitzgerald!" Savage called sharply. The two sophomores came up eagerly and went out to replace Glass and Crump. The quarterback obviously needed a rest and Savage wanted a word or two with Vince.

Rolph made Glass lie down and threw a blanket over him, although Al protested that he was all right, merely shaken up.

"Was there a fight?" he asked, eyes alight.

"Almost, but never mind that," Savage advised him. "You do as Dave says and take it easy. We'll need you later, boy. You've been calling them like a wizard."

To Crump, he said coldly: "Keep your temper under control, Vince. We nearly had a free-for-all."

"My temper?" the guard replied in fiery fashion. "Did you hear that crowd yelling for 'em to get me? And that tramp clobbers Al! They're the ones spoiling for the fight, not us!"

There was enough truth in the protest to keep Savage from answering in the same heated vein. Although his warning to the team before the game had been clear and unmistakable, he could not in all fairness bench Crump for the flare-up. There had been provocation.

"All right, so you hit someone," Savage retorted. "Whether he slugged you first makes no difference — you'll be tossed. What good will you do the club on the bench? We've got fourteen points on this outfit and they're beat

63

right now if we just play football. How about it?"

Crump squared his big shoulders.

"O.K.," he said grudgingly. "Shall I go in now?"

"In a minute. I want to see how Fitz makes out. Get off your feet and cool down."

He turned away with the feeling that once more he had come out second best with Vince. If Fitzgerald held up, he'd give Crump plenty of time to cool down.

Fitzgerald, game but inexperienced, could not get the job done. Hammering at Casper's spot, the Braves jolted to two first downs quickly, and when LaCosta called down to warn that Casper looked used up, Savage had no choice but to send Crump back. He replaced Casper with Battman, another green guard, and he knew that Vince's line backer support was needed.

As the quarter ended, Linfield moved across the Hastings 30. The play was hard, but not visibly rough. The Braves wanted a score to get back into contention; vengeance could wait.

The Cavaliers held on the 12, thanks to a break. With fourth and a yard to go, the Linfield left tackle either missed or anticipated the starting signal. Before the center had snapped the ball, he had charged across the line into Battman, knocking him flat. It cost the Braves five yards, and Rose almost made it on the next try, but not quite.

Savage pulled out his other hard-used starters to give them a breather, but they did not stay on the side lines long. Hastings made one first down as Kassowitz fooled the end on a bootleg play, but the Linfield line smothered every other attempt and Glass went in to punt.

"We're not going to run this outfit, are we?" Savage said wryly to Breck.

"Let 'em have the first downs," was George's reply. "Look at the scoreboard."

Linfield continued to amass the first downs. Four in succession this time, then Crump, shooting the gap on third down, hit Morris before he could get the ball away. Again Hastings' offensive efforts proved futile, to Savage's chagrin, and again Glass kicked out of danger.

Savage looked at the clock. With only five minutes remaining and sixty yards to go, the Braves, who had not tried a single pass, would have to take to the air now. He sent in Schmidt, his third fullback, with a word of warning to beware the long ones. The Cavaliers had drilled all week against two particular patterns Linfield had shown as Bassich scouted them.

The Braves produced one of those patterns immediately. Morris swept to his right as though on the option play, then tossed out to the halfback, who threw on the dead run to the end, cutting toward the outside.

Travis scented it. He flashed in front of the intended receiver, made the interception without changing stride, and winged upfield. It was a very dangerous move on Junior's part, for had he missed, Linfield had an almost certain touchdown.

But he did not miss, and no Brave laid a hand on him during his forty yard race to the goal line.

Savage found himself screaming like a schoolboy and embracing the person next to him at the moment, who turned out to be Dave Rolph. The trainer was yelling too.

" There goes your ball game! " Ed shouted gleefully.

The fact that Whitney missed this try for point did not seem to matter. A 20–0 lead at half time was a huge insurance policy.

Dr. Beardsley went to the Linfield dressing room during the intermission and returned with the information that Haggerty had been taken to a hospital as a precautionary measure. The Braves' physician thought he might have a slight concussion, and preferred to take no chances.

"I don't suppose Waterman is very happy about that," Savage sighed.

"Tough break," LaCosta agreed soberly. "If they'd scored on that first drive, we might be three behind instead of 20–0. Now, we've got it made, especially if they don't score the first time they get the ball."

The Braves made a desperate try. They hammered down to the 19 on three- and four-yard smashes at the Hastings center, but Hearst stopped the fourth-down slant buck inches short and again the Cavaliers took over on downs.

Abruptly, the temper of the game changed. Two plays later, Crump emerged with blood trickling from his nose. Glass punted, and Linfield was charged with clipping on the runback. The stands broke loose again. Twice the Braves' quarterback had to signal his own rooters for quiet so that his voice could be heard.

Then a Braves' blocker kept trying to push Clawson aside after a play had ended, and finally Bob grabbed him by the jersey and spun him roughly to the turf. The Brave bounced up, obviously full of fight, but a teammate grabbed him and pulled him away. Clawson jawed at him, and when Travis said something, the center shook his head angrily.

Savage turned quickly and called, "Murdock!"

The second-string center jumped to his feet.

"Never mind, Bill," Savage said, and Murdock sat down, disappointed. Savage's face was drawn in taut lines, and his mind was a turmoil of indecision. He could see the explosion point drawing nearer with every play, and his first reaction had been to remove Clawson at once. But like Crump, the center had been given some provocation. Savage realized that he might have done the same thing himself had a blocker tried that trick on him.

He went to the press-box phone.

"Can you see what's going on out there, Sam?"

"Plenty, but it's like watching a dogfight under a blanket. You can tell something's happening, but not exactly what. I've seen some fist work in the line."

"Ours?"

"A few. The officials are either blind or white-livered. They're not calling one tenth the stuff."

Savage looked at the clock, saw the third quarter was half gone. If he replaced his starters, the hard-nosed ones, maybe Linfield would calm down. It seemed the only way to avert a serious outbreak, and he was sure that Linfield could not score three times in the time remaining. He began to call off names.

"You putting in an entire team, Ed?" Breck asked worriedly. "Our kids don't look tired."

"I know it, but I don't want any fights."

"But it's Linfield that's acting up," the assistant protested. Savage did not reply. He was busy instructing Kassowitz.

The regulars came off reluctantly. Clawson's upper lip was puffed; Crump had a swollen nose and a lump under one eye; Mahoney had a cut on his nose and skin off his knuckles.

"I'll get that Clymer or die trying," he vowed loudly, flinging his helmet on the ground.

Savage, his eyes troubled, pretended he had not heard. The time did not seem auspicious for a lecture on sportsmanship.

"What did you say to Clawson?" he asked Junior Travis, who laughed mirthlessly.

"I told him to keep his head screwed on, and I thought he was going to hit me. He wanted to hit somebody, sure."

Savage thought of Marty Regan's words — " I don't know

67

what luck you'll have making them change."

Out on the field, the Hastings second string was resisting doggedly, but Linfield was moving again. Faced with easier opposition, the Braves forgot private feuds and went for the touchdown.

They made it on the second play of the fourth quarter, and it seemed to ignite them. Behind now, 20–7, they hurled back three feeble Cavalier attempts after the kickoff, took Kassowitz' short punt on their 35, and started downfield again.

" Hadn't we better get the first string back in? " George Breck asked anxiously.

Again indecision gripped Savage. Then a Linfield runner broke clear at center and raced past mid-field before the plucky Kassowitz pulled him down.

He made up his mind at that moment. Whether Hastings won by two touchdowns or one point made little difference, but it was important that the Cavaliers win. Important to him. Let Linfield watch its own manners. He was not going to throw away victory for what seemed, at the moment, a principle that could not be defended. The regulars were going back.

Their return was met with prolonged booing.

" They love it," Breck said, his thin face lighting up. " They love the rough going. Watch 'em cool those Braves."

And so they did, although Linfield knocked off one more first down before the Cavaliers held. Crump and Hearst hit Rose at the same time, and hard. The weary halfback had to be assisted from the field, and again the " Get 66 " chant went up from the Linfield rooters.

Let 'em howl, Savage thought fiercely, and was startled by his own ferocity. He was getting as bad as the rooting section, he realized. And two hours ago he had delivered a speech on clean play! The scent of victory was a heady perfume.

Travis came swinging wide around end, picked up four yards, and was stopped. Two Braves piled on top of him in a manner so obviously vengeful that Savage raced out on the field and had to be waved back by Ogden. Travis sat on the grass, gripping his ankle, as Ogden paced off fifteen yards against Linfield for unnecessary roughness.

Travis came off limping.

"Turned under me," he explained, gasping, to Savage's concerned inquiry.

If the Cavaliers lost Travis, Savage thought bitterly, this victory would come high. He left Junior to the ministrations of Doc Beardsley and went back to his restless pacing in front of the bench.

Glass laid a beautiful punt out of bounds inside the Linfield 10 and Savage, checking the clock again swiftly, decided that the Cavaliers had bought enough time to win. There was no percentage in getting any more regulars racked up.

They came out looking battered, but not beaten. Crump had a discolored eye to go with his puffed nose, but he seemed quite exhilarated, like a fighter who had won a hard match. Mahoney confided happily to Clawson, "That Clymer will remember *me*, I'll bet you!" and Whitney was fingering a swollen hand gingerly.

There was no more rough stuff, nor was there any scoring in the few minutes remaining. Linfield was badly used up too, and, even against the Cavalier reserves, had difficulty working itself out of the hole into which Glass had kicked it.

Savage heard the welcome final gun with curiously mixed feelings. His exuberance at the smashing upset was undercut by his uneasy dissatisfaction with the manner in which it had been scored. It did not mean, he assured himself, that he was retreating from the standards he had set. But in extreme cases, one had to fight fire with fire.

As he walked across the field for the perfunctory handshake with a sullen Len Waterman, he wished fervently that it had not been necessary.

He was in no mood to mouth polite phrases to the Linfield coach; they did little more than touch fingers and turn away. He was further depressed by Dr. Beardsley's estimate that Travis' twisted ankle, while not serious, might not permit him to play the following Saturday.

" I wish we were leaving for home right now instead of tomorrow morning," he said somberly as the coaches were dressing. " I've seen all of this place I can use today."

" The boys need a little relaxation after a game like this, Ed," Breck said. " So do you, I'd guess. You don't seem very happy, and it was a big win, believe me."

Savage's blond features relaxed a little. He had been grousing around like a loser, he had to admit.

"Well, sure, but let's not kid ourselves about our offense," Savage remarked. "We ain't got no offense. Did you look at the statistics? We made four first downs. I don't know how many they made, but it seemed like forty."

" Give the defense the credit, then," Breck advised gaily. " Take the win any way you can get it, eh, Sam? "

"Any way at all," LaCosta said blandly. Savage gave him a quick glance. Was there a hidden barb there? He could not be sure.

After dinner, the players were on their own until eleven o'clock. Savage would have liked to turn in early, but he and Sam could hardly lock the door of their room against such visitors as Cal Murchison, Jake Gledhill, and a number of enthusiastic alumni, including one who was willing to back Savage for President.

Murchison was the last to leave, shortly before eleven.

"On to the Rose Bowl, Ed," he said happily as he went out. "I'm beginning to believe it."

Savage grinned at Sam as the door closed.

"Rose Bowl? We'll pay to get in there, and Cal knows it. He'll come down off that cloud in the morning. Well, me for the sack, Sambo."

Savage was brushing his teeth when the telephone rang.

"Get that, will you, Sam?" he called.

He heard LaCosta say, "Yes, this is his room." Then, in a shocked voice: "What? What for? For the — Wait a minute. Where's the station? Sixteenth and Clay? He'll be right down."

Savage hustled out of the bathroom. Sam was putting down the phone with a dazed look.

"That was the desk sergeant at the Tenth Precinct," he said slowly. "There's been a fight. They've got Crump and Clawson down there."

6

THE desk sergeant at the Tenth Precinct, red-faced and bald, was as cheerful as the airless, dark-paneled room was cheerless. He greeted Savage and LaCosta with a chuckle.

"Mr. Savage, is it? There are your two hearties over there."

Two figures rose from a bench in the darkened corner of the room and advanced toward the desk. Both were wearing the team traveling jackets, red with a white "Cavaliers" woven on one side. Clawson's sandy hair was mussed and he looked a bit apprehensive when he saw the coaches' unsmiling faces. But Crump was completely self-possessed.

"Hi, Coach; hello, Sam," he said. "Had a small ruckus. Sorry they had to call you in."

Even in the uncertain light cast by the bulbs on the sergeant's desk, the white scar on Vince's cheek stood out clearly. The combat infantryman, Savage thought, afraid of nothing. But this was not Korea.

"What happened, Vince? What's the charge?"

The sergeant answered, chuckling again.

"No charges, Mr. Savage. Not against these two. We're holding four others who don't look no better than yours.

72

They started it, it seems, and these boys of yours was merely defending themselves. Did pretty good, too, though you can see they got marked up a mite."

"Sergeant," Crump said with a flash of his fine teeth, "not one of those heroes laid a hand on me or my friend. The marks you see on us are from the great American game of football."

"Are they now?" the sergeant asked in pretended amazement. "It must be a grand sport, then."

"They're free to go?" asked Savage.

"Free as air. I called you just to make sure they got home without no further — ah — unpleasantness. In case they are attacked again, I mean."

"Thank you, Sergeant," Savage said in grateful relief. "Let's go, men."

Outside, he flagged a taxi. Crump explained, with an occasional reference to Clawson for corroboration. They had just strolled downtown, ending their wanderings in a hamburger place. A group of four in the restaurant — "Linfield redhots," Crump said contemptuously — followed them outside and one asked Vince if his name was Crump.

"I said it was, and just like that, the four of them jumped us. It didn't last long. But we were lucky, because a patrol car happened to be passing. The two cops saw the start of it and knew it wasn't our fault. They booked the other guys, though, including one who has a busted nose or I never saw one. That about it, Bob?"

"That's the way it was, Big Dog." Clawson sounded admiring.

LaCosta spoke for the first time.

"'Man is born to trouble as the sparks fly upward,'" he quoted, with a rueful smile. "You're sure an upward-flying spark, Vince."

Crump said steadily: "I don't look for trouble, Sam.

But if it looks for me, I don't run. What would you have done?"

"He'd fight," Savage interposed heavily. "I'm just sorry it happened. You're sure both of you are all right? You didn't get banged up any more?"

"By those kids?" Clawson had regained his assurance. "Vince could have handled the lot of them alone."

"Look, fellows," Savage tried to sound jocular, "when we get to the hotel, go to your rooms and stay there until our bus leaves for the airport tomorrow. Take breakfast upstairs; I'll pay for it myself. And don't bump into anybody crossing the lobby, please."

"Not unless they bump into us first, Coach," Crump said with a crooked grin.

"Of all the guys on the squad who had to get in a fight," Savage remarked with a helpless air when he and Sam reached their own rooms, "it had to be those two. And yet it wasn't their fault."

"It wasn't their fault today, either, Ed. It's just the nature of the beast — Vince, I mean. He doesn't make trouble deliberately, but it sure travels with him. And of course, fellows like Clawson and Mahoney and Hearst and a lot of others look up to him. I don't like it much."

"Neither do I, Sam." Savage had the feeling that La-Costa was asking him what he was going to do about Crump. And at the moment, he was not prepared to do anything.

Perhaps LaCosta guessed what was in his thoughts, for he veered off at a tangent.

"Are you going to call Murchison?"

"Oof!" He hadn't given Cal a thought. "I suppose I'd better — no, I won't. Why spoil his sleep too?"

"He'd like it better hearing it from you than reading it in the papers tomorrow morning," Sam pointed out.

74

Savage pondered that a moment.

"I'll gamble, Sam. Crump and Clawson aren't on the police blotter, because they weren't booked. And it's fairly late. Unless the sergeant calls the papers himself, they may not get it at all. Anyway, not tonight. I'll have to tell Jake Gledhill, of course, but he won't use it if no one else does, I'm sure. And we'll be out of town by ten tomorrow morning."

So he let Murchison sleep, not entirely unselfishly. His own brain was much too weary to welcome a session with the athletic director at that moment.

As a gamble, it proved a good one. The newspapers carried nothing on the altercation, although the game stories in both made Savage scowl in anger. That Hastings had been lucky to win, he admitted freely. But without making the direct charge of rough or dirty play by the Cavaliers, each writer laid heavy stress on the early injury to Haggerty and made several references to the game of the preceding season. But nowhere in any account was there mention of the Linfield rooting section or the numerous penalties incurred by the Braves.

"They don't give us much, do they, Sam?" Savage said. "I'm just grateful they didn't know about last night."

He was pleasantly surprised by Murchison's reaction.

"Oh, no!" Cal groaned at the news. But when he had heard the whole story, his anxiety lessened, and soon he was philosophical about it.

"I suppose it will come out — those stories always do. And some of our friends" — he gave Savage a meaningful look — "won't like it. Another black eye for Hastings, they'll say. But it's certainly no reflection on the school or you or the boys. It wasn't their fault, obviously."

Jake Gledhill agreed that it would not look good in print.

" Not in this town, anyway. Have you seen the papers, Ed? "

Savage said grimly that he had.

" Don't look so mad," Gledhill counseled cheerily. " What did you expect for beating the home-town favorite after the build-up for this game? "

The trip home was a noisy one. To the squad's natural exuberance over victory was now added the spice of the Crump-Clawson exploit, gleefully related by both. That it added to their stature in their teammates' eyes was quite evident.

" I wish I'd been along — " Larry Hearst said wistfully, adding, " not that you needed me."

But that manifestation of hero worship did not concern Savage nearly so much as the prospect of facing St. Vincent's the next weekend without the services of Junior Travis. Doc Beardsley, examining the ankle that morning, was definitely pessimistic.

" The best thing I can see," Savage told LaCosta and Breck, " is to move Freeman from fullback to left half. At least he can pass, and we could get more out of that 22 series."

The one thing Travis could not do was throw a football. He had small hands, and after a few days of watching his scatter-arm efforts, Savage had abandoned the attempt to make a swan out of a duck. It did limit the Cavalier offense to a degree, in that it precluded the use of the checkoff passing play from the left half when Travis was in the game. But Junior's other abilities more than compensated for it, the coaches agreed.

Behind Travis, the best bets were Clampett, a senior who was adequate, but no more, and McLain, a light-weight tricky-stepping sophomore of considerable promise, but green. Neither could be called a good passer, and the switching of Freeman appeared the best possible solution.

To Savage's gratification, the plane was met at the airport by a small but enthusiastic knot of rooters who echoed Cal Murchison's chant of " On to the Rose Bowl," and even wangled a short, embarrassed acknowledgment from Savage himself in the terminal building.

" That Rose Bowl stuff is getting on my nerves," he confessed to LaCosta. " We win two games and we're in Pasadena. Somebody is building up to a mighty fall."

" First thing you know they'll be calling you the Boy Wonder Coach," Sam said slyly. " That's the kiss of death."

" I expect to be called worse before I'm through."

And he was, the next morning.

His hope that Saturday night's postgame fight would escape official notice proved vain. On Monday morning, the Linfield student sports editor came out with a searing column headed " Savage's Savages."

A somewhat apologetic Associated Press man from the local bureau read the column to Savage over the phone.

" ' A new coach, but the same old tactics,' " it began. " ' It's an open secret that Jim Trainor left Hastings because coaches were tired of having their teams beaten up physically by his roughnecks from the coal-mining country. But Saturday's game here revealed that the new coach, Ed Savage, is simply carrying on in the Trainor (or shall we say Hastings?) tradition. Not five minutes had passed before Jimmy Haggerty was carried from the field with a brain concussion after being hit by Vince Crump, the Cavaliers' chief hatchet man. Later, Crump tried to pick a fight with Milt Sloan, Linfield end, and to cap it all, Crump and another Hastings savage, Bob Clawson, got into a fight in downtown Linfield Saturday night.

" ' I say, let's refuse to play Hastings in football again

until it abandons what I call " Savagery " and cleans up its game. . . . ' "

There was much more in the same vehement style.

" Naturally, we'd like your comment on it," the A.P. man said warily when he had finished. Savage, his hand gripping the phone so hard that his knuckles showed white, counted five to himself before replying. Outraged though he was, he knew he would gain nothing by an intemperate exchange with a student.

" The boy sounds a little worked up," he said at last. " Has anyone asked Len Waterman's opinion of the way the game was played? "

The A.P. man said the Linfield bureau had called Waterman, who disclaimed any knowledge of the column and did not care to comment.

A nice duck, Savage thought acidly. Len could have squashed it with one sentence had he so desired. Instead, he was permitting an undergraduate to voice what he did not dare. Savage had little doubt that the source of the column lay higher than the sports editor, and that intensified his bitterness.

" Anyone who saw the game knows the accusation is without foundation," he said, his voice crackling. " I was sorry to see Haggerty hurt, but anyone interested is welcome to look at our movies of the play. It was a hard tackle, nothing else.

" As for the fight, my two players were defending themselves against an unprovoked attack. The police absolved them of all blame; why shouldn't I? That's all I care to say on the subject."

The A.P. man was obviously not satisfied with the brief reply. He had more questions, but Savage remained courteously firm. He would provide no fuel for this controversy if he could help it.

It did not end there, however. The Linfield papers picked it up, which impelled Jake Gledhill to throw off restraint and use his column to berate not only the Braves but the Linfield press as well.

Savage was both hurt and bewildered by the storm of charge and countercharge involving him.

"I've never been in anything like this before," he told Murchison. "And it's absolutely unfair!"

"Ed, don't let it upset you that much," Cal reassured him. "I've made it clear to the Board that it's merely a petty way of face-saving by Patrick and Waterman. They're both boiling about losing. And when Waterman popped off last year about not playing us again, I had to get pretty firm with Linfield. I suppose that rankles too."

So the members of the Athletic Board had been asking questions, Savage thought in dismay.

"Anyway, it will be good for the gate," Murchison went on with a facetious air. "We'll probably draw forty thousand Saturday. How are the boys reacting to all this nonsense about how rough they are?"

"With more amusement than anything else," Savage admitted ruefully. "Some of them think 'Savage's Savages' is real cute," he added and laughed.

"If that's their attitude, we'll beat St. Vincent's."

St. Vincent's gave Hastings a good licking.

Savage sensed the Cavaliers were in for trouble as early as Wednesday. The squad seemed unaccountably flat, and the workout, the first hard one of the week, had been, in LaCosta's opinion, the worst of the season.

By Friday night, Savage was devoid of confidence.

"What is it?" he asked in harried perplexity. "They're trying hard enough, but they're not accomplishing a thing. Why should Whitney drop three easy passes?"

"I think they're still playing Linfield," LaCosta said.

" They got worked up pretty high for that one."

" It's not all mental," Breck put in. " We got a good going-over physically too. Bound to be some reaction."

They were both right, Savage knew. The Linfield game had taken its toll in more ways than one. But perhaps the Cavaliers would come up a bit on game day.

They did not. Savage knew it in the dressing room, recognizing the indefinable sense of not quite being with it. He had known times like it himself, games for which he could not really rouse himself. Whether it had been emotional or physical exhaustion, he could not tell. But there was little a coach could do to recharge human batteries under those circumstances. He wasted no time trying.

That it would have been wasted effort was apparent from the outset when Glass, running the bootleg play, inexplicably dropped the ball without being touched. Savage stifled a groan and prepared for a long day of it.

It was nothing he could pinpoint. There was no reason why Clawson should hit a runner at the line of scrimmage and then let him slither away for a twelve-yard gain. Or for Maderas to drop a pass from Freeman in the clear, or for Corbett to miss a signal and foul up a deep reverse when the Cavaliers were striking for a touchdown on the Saints' 15-yard line.

All those happened, and more. Not for lack of trying. The Cavaliers fought doggedly, but without the explosive spark of the previous week. Len Waterman was getting a measure of revenge, though in a secondhand way.

There were some exceptions. Crump roamed the defensive secondary with cold efficiency, making tackle after tackle. Larry Hearst, despite being badly suckered on trap plays two or three times, still wrecked a number of shots at his side of the line by smashing in with abandon. And Freeman, though lacking Travis' jolting impact, performed acceptably in his unfamiliar role of halfback. His long run led up to a Hastings touchdown late in the second period, but Whitney missed on the extra point and St. Vincent's led at the half, 14–6.

The Saints had scored once on a sustained drive, once on a long pass when Glass and Freeman mixed up their defensive assignments and let a receiver get behind them.

The second half was no better. When the Saints tallied again in the third quarter for 21–6, Savage bleakly conceded defeat to himself. He began to substitute freely and St. Vincent's added one more touchdown before it ended.

Some of the reserves, notably a stringy junior end named Bedolla, played above Savage's expectations. That was only sugar-coating on the pill of defeat, however.

Still, he tried to sound an optimistic note in the subdued atmosphere of the dressing room.

" All right, men, let's get our daubers up again. That was the bad one we had to get out of our systems. There are five more to play. Next week we'll give Burnside the time of its life."

At the moment, the players, depressed and disgusted, obviously did not believe it. Nor did Savage. But he began to feel a little better as he moved about to talk to individuals.

Al Glass approached him and said in a shaky voice: " I lost the game today, Coach. I was terrible."

Savage saw the boy was close to tears. He slapped him on the back.

" Don't talk nonsense, Al. We got beat, that's all. You're the best quarterback in the league. Without you, we'd be 0–3 right now, and I mean that."

Glass gave him a searching look, then, said, " O.K., thanks," and turned away. Then Tony Corbett, looking equally miserable, offered apologies for his misplays, real and imaginary.

"The worst game I've ever had," he lamented in self-recrimination. It took Savage a few minutes to talk him around. These were the first indications that either boy had regarded him as anything but an impersonal figure, the head coach. Yet both had displayed a sense of letting him down by their mistakes. Not the coach, but Ed Savage, the person.

That gave his flagging spirits a lift. He was even able to laugh outright at the interview with the newsmen when Roy Caster, the student sports editor, blurted, "Well, nobody can accuse us of rough play today, that's certain."

When the chuckles had subsided, Jake Gledhill inquired if Savage planned any major changes in the line-up.

"Whom would I change, Jake? Except for Travis, that was our best team out there, and it just wasn't good enough today. I don't think shifting it around would help much."

Gledhill grunted, seemed about to say something, but did not.

Cal Murchison was downcast, but not gloomy.

"There goes my pipe dream about a share of the Rose Bowl gate," he commented, then smiled to show he was joking. "I admit I didn't think we'd lose this one, but the boys will bounce back."

It would require some bounce to rise above Burnside, Savage thought, but Cal knew that perfectly well. Right now, Savage preferred to pretend he had never heard of Burnside, and contemplate the more pleasant prospect of his date the next day with Sarah Fleming.

7

ED, what kind of man was Jim Trainor? "

Sarah Fleming put the question without preliminaries, catching Savage by surprise. It was an unusually warm mid-October day, and they had abandoned a rather aimless drive in the hills back of the campus to sit under a huge oak tree.

" Why, I don't know, doll. I never met the man."

" I met him once." Sarah's brown eyes were thoughtful. " I didn't like him. His ear lobes were too big."

"Well, that's logical. Man with big ear lobes, strictly no good. Can't fool a woman when it comes to character."

"Don't make fun of me. It's true I didn't like him on sight, and I was right, wasn't I? He wasn't a nice man."

Savage, who had been leaning lazily against the tree trunk and regarding Sarah fondly, sat up.

"Look, what started this? " he asked in bewilderment. " You and Jim Trainor? "

" If you must know, I've been reading the sports pages. I admit I don't understand all of it, but they've been comparing you to Jim Trainor in a very uncomplimentary way, haven't they? It made me mad to read it. I wish you'd explain it to me."

"Aw, Sarah," he protested, frowning, "it's a long, dull,

complicated story, and besides, I don't want to gab about football. Not to you. Not today."

"Please, Ed. I really do want to know."

So as briefly as he could, he outlined the situation confronting him, his approach to it, and the disheartening backlash from the Linfield game.

"You see," he concluded, smiling, "big ear lobes are merely incidental. I suppose it's the old truism of giving a dog a bad name."

"What you really need is a brand-new dog."

"Lacking same, I must teach them new tricks. Or make 'em forget some of the old ones. Now for goodness' sake, let's find another subject."

"Not quite yet," she said somberly. "I'm not exactly a little ray of sunshine this afternoon, but I think I ought to mention this, Ed. Your boy McLain, is he a valuable player?"

"Jerry? Not now. Next year, maybe. He's only a soph."

"I know," she said with a hint of exasperation. "I have him three days a week in English 2. At least, he comes to class, but he hasn't done much work. I'm afraid he's headed for probation at mid-term."

"Oh-oh. That bad?"

"It's not that he's dull-witted. I can work with a boy who has trouble with English, and you'd be astounded how many bright ones are paralyzed by the prospect of writing a simple declarative sentence. But Jerry hasn't turned in half the assignments. If he doesn't make them up in the next three weeks, I'll have to report him to the dean."

"I'll talk to the kid tomorrow," Savage said. "And I appreciate your telling me, so don't look so forlorn. Football players have to do the work, same as anyone else. I know I did."

"I've heard that some of them haven't, Ed," she said pointedly.

Savage was taken aback. He recalled Murchison's reluctant admission that entrance requirements had been waived for some of Trainor's recruits. It was understandable that a soft ride in the classroom might follow.

"I don't know anything about it, Sarah," he said with a grimace. "As far as I'm concerned, my players have to cut it or else."

He tackled McLain next day before practice.

The sophomore, a slender youngster with a bright, confident manner, appeared more defiant than worried.

"That stuff," he muttered. "I can't write those themes. Why should I try to be an author when I'm going to be an engineer?"

"Jerry, maybe you can become a good engineer even if you can't sign your own name, though I doubt it. But one thing is certain — you have to pass English 2 before you graduate from Hastings, and you might as well do it this semester. Besides, if you make probation, you can't play football. So pull up your socks and get caught up on those themes. Promise?"

McLain promised, a bit sulkily. Savage made a mental note to check with Sarah in a week's time.

He approached the practice field with some trepidation. You could tell, from the chatter, on that first day after a humiliating defeat, whether a team would remain prostrate or try to get up. It wasn't an infallible system, but it was an indicator. A quiet team was usually a dispirited one.

As Savage stepped into the enclosure, he heard noise, lots of it, from the scattered groups engaged in impromptu warmups. As he reached for the whistle to signal the start of the session, he smiled faintly. There was hope.

Whether motivated by wounded pride or disgust with their performance against the Saints, Savage could not be sure, but the squad was obviously eager for the Burnside game. On Wednesday, he kept them working until the floodlights were needed, and there were cries of " Just one more, Coach," when he finally called it off.

" They're certainly in better fettle for this one," LaCosta said with satisfaction. " Did you hear Mahoney out there? He was talking it up like a cheerleader. Usually he won't open his face."

" It's strange," Savage observed, wonderingly. " This isn't a ' hubba hubba ' club, either. It doesn't have any real holler guys."

" This bunch never has been much for that," Breck commented. " It's more like a pro outfit in that respect."

Savage saw LaCosta's lips twitch. George had spoken quite guilelessly, but the reference to pros obviously amused Sam.

Jake Gledhill, looking more rumpled than ever, was waiting for Savage after Thursday's workout, inquiring about line-up changes. Ed repeated that there would be none.

Jake chewed meditatively on his pencil.

" You know, Ed, Trainor would have chewed this club good after last Saturday and turned the line-up upside down. I admire the way you're doing the job, considering what you're up against."

" Well, thanks, Jake." Savage was mystified. " What do you mean, what I'm up against? "

Gledhill gave him a look over the top of his glasses.

" Look, I'm a Hastings man myself, and I've been covering the Cavaliers for eighteen years. You stepped into a mess here, and don't tell me you didn't know it."

" You make it sound a lot worse than it is," Savage

sparred. He did not know what Jake was leading up to.
" It's nothing that six more animals wouldn't fix."

" Exactly. And where do you think you're going to get
'em? Next year and the year after, I mean? "

" From the usual sources, naturally. There are a lot of
high schools in this state."

" And only so many good athletes, you know that."

" We've always gotten our share," Savage said, and
thought of Marty Regan. He'd bring Marty back into the
fold, and the others like him.

Gledhill made a scornful noise.

" Are you kidding, Ed? One of the reasons Jim Trainor
was hired was the fact that Hastings wasn't getting its
share of the prep nuggets — or anyway, what it needed to
compete on even terms with the rest of the league. It was
losing the kids who like to play for a winner, and the ones
that didn't have the grades but could get in elsewhere,
and the ones that needed financial help. You don't get
one third the football scholarships available to Rossiter
or Mount Royal, do you? "

Savage said he was aware of that, but —

" But what? " Gledhill demanded. " Trainor's gone and
the gravy train is derailed. Even the booster clubs that
used to slip a boy a few extra bucks if he needed it are
dead now. So Hastings is right where it was when it let
Pappy go. I think it ought to get out of the Conference."

" What? "

" I mean it." Gledhill was deadly serious. " I've told Cal
that several times. The league's outgrown the school. Or
maybe it's the other way round. But we can't play the big
ones even unless we proselyte in a big way. The Board
tried that and now it wishes it hadn't."

" We'll play with students, then," Savage said jocularly.
" If the Board wasn't prepared to have Hastings lose a

few, it would have gone for a name coach, instead of me. That's obvious."

"Win a few, lose a few, eh?" Jake replied cynically. "Sure, that's their attitude now, and Murchison's too. They mean it. But for every alumnus who doesn't care much about the football team, there are three who grouse and grumble and write letters to the papers and to the trustees and to the prexy every time Hastings loses to Rossiter. No matter what Cal thinks, they don't like losing. Who do you think fired Pappy? The alumni, that's who."

Savage made a little gesture of resignation.

"Jake, you make me wonder why I ever took this job." Gledhill sighed.

"When I get on my pet hobbyhorse, I ride it too far," he confessed, looking contrite. "I'd hate to see you walk into one, that's all. Now, what about Saturday? Are you going to unhook those Vikings?"

They talked about the Burnside game, but Savage's mind was still assimilating Jake's speech. There were bits and pieces of recognizable truth in it, but he thought that Gledhill's picture was badly distorted. And he was certain of one thing — Cal Murchison had not picked him to steer the Cavaliers into gridiron oblivion. "A representative team is what we want," Murchison had said. They would get it.

In that sense, a "representative team" could not be expected to beat Burnside. The Vikings were coming in as two-touchdown favorites. They did not possess a grinding running game like Linfield, but they were nicely balanced between offensive and defensive strength, with a fine triple-threat halfback named Watkins.

"You know, we might just do it," Savage told his assistants Friday night. "If our pass defense holds up, that's all.

They're a pretty strong outfit running inside, but that's our strength too."

" I promised Hearst that if they trap him more than once on the cutback, I'd beat his brains out with a spoon," La-Costa said.

" I thought we looked better on offense this week than we have all year, Ed," Breck put in. " Frankly, last Saturday night, I didn't think we had much chance, but the way the kids have come up, can do."

They were loose in the dressing room, full of jokes and horseplay, and eager to get on the field. After he had gone over the play diagrams on the blackboard, Savage addressed the squad.

" You know you can play better ball than you did last week," he said. " So do I. Why not prove it to your rooters? All right, Al, take 'em out."

Glass, the game captain, led the file, yelling and whooping, through the tunnel and onto the turf.

Savage, pacing in front of the bench, knew from the first play that his hunch had been right. Burnside tried the cutback at Hearst's slot, but the sophomore, deftly using a forearm shiver to fight off the cross block, pulled Watkins down with a high tackle.

Then the Viking halfback swung to his right on the run-pass option play, and Maderas sliced in from behind so fast that Watkins had to go wide and Mahoney cracked him for two lost.

" They're up," Savage said out of the side of his mouth to Breck. " Keep your fingers crossed."

Sturdy as the Cavalier defense proved during the first period, it was no stronger than Burnside's. With Freeman at fullback, Savage had hoped to loosen the visitors' defense by the double passing threat. But Burnside did a smart job of covering receivers as well as blanketing Travis. Obviously, the Viking scouts had returned with the information that Junior was the runner to fear. Once or twice he was able to smash inside for nice gains as Crump and Hearst cleared a path through the rugged Burnside front rank, but he could not shake loose outside.

Savage could see that Whitney, who was supposed to take the defensive halfback on the strong side sweep, wasn't doing it. But from his restricted observation point in front of the bench, he could not tell why. He was about to pull the end out to question him when LaCosta called.

"You have to adjust on that 22 sweep, Ed. They've got Junior tabbed as no passer, and the halfback comes up as soon as he sees Travis has the ball. That's why Whit isn't getting to him in time."

Savage chewed at his underlip. The sweep series was a cornerstone of the Cavalier attack, and Travis was the one who made it go.

"We could let Maderas take the halfback and send Whit after the safety," he said, keeping his eyes on the field where Glass was dropping back into punt formation. "After all, Sid's a decoy on that play, and if he isn't decoying anyone, he might as well knock somebody down."

"I've got a better idea." Sam sounded just a bit excited. "Let Junior throw one."

"Sam, he can't throw as well as you can," Savage protested. "You know that; you've watched him! Two to one it would be intercepted."

"By whom?" LaCosta sounded really excited now, like a fisherman with a big one on his line. "You could shoot deer behind that halfback, he comes up so fast. And they don't rotate all the way to cover against the pass. They're sold Junior isn't going to throw. Shucks, have him fling it out of bounds if you want, but you've got to keep that

90

halfback honest or forget the play, Ed."

"Well," Savage began dubiously, and then decided to buy it. Sam was right; the halfback had to be kept honest. It was worth the risk to give Travis a little running room.

"You're on, Sambo," he said crisply. " Live dangerously, that's our motto."

George Breck batted his eyes when Savage told him.

"Kill or cure, eh?" His uncertain laugh revealed his misgivings, but after all, Savage was the boss.

With Burnside deep in its own territory, Savage substituted Kassowitz and Clampett for Glass and Travis. He wanted to brief the latter pair first rather than send in the play from the bench. Junior's shortcomings as a passer had been the object of much joking on the quad and Savage wanted him to understand the strategy.

If Travis was at all nervous at the prospect, he did not show it. Glass looked surprised, then grinned.

"Remember, Junior, don't throw it to me," he joshed. "I'll be behind you."

Travis rammed an elbow into the quarterback's ribs.

"Don't try it until you're past our 40, Al," Savage said. "Whitney is the deep man, Junior. If he's covered, throw the ball out of bounds or eat it, and we'll try it another time."

Noise from the bench and the Hastings stands wrenched their attention back to the gridiron, where Crump had just shot the gap to kill a delayed fullback spinner for a loss. Burnside called time out for the fullback, who had the wind knocked out of him.

"That Vince," Glass said admiringly. "I'm glad I'm on his side. He hurts."

Travis said nothing. After Burnside had kicked to the Cavalier 32, Savage sent the two back into the line-up.

The fullback hold-off worked for the first time that day,

and Glass got a big eight yards outside right tackle. Then Freeman knifed over guard for the first down, and as the Hastings rooters came alive, Savage tugged nervously at his shirt collar. If Glass followed orders, this would be the 22 pass. For a moment, he wished he had shut his ears to LaCosta's brilliant suggestion, but it was too late.

He knew that as Glass spun and handed off and Travis, with Crump and Sonny Caspar leading him, sprinted wide for the Vikings' left.

The Burnside halfback came up as though magnetized, and on the edge of his vision Savage saw Whitney feint a block on the safety and then veer to his right. The safety went with him for two strides, then let him go as he ascertained that the ball carrier was Travis.

Junior stopped suddenly, cocked his arm, and threw. It was a wobbly, broken-backed pass that traveled no more than thirty yards. To Savage, watching agonizedly, it seemed to hang in the air for at least thirty seconds. But when it finally came down, five yards from the side line, only Whitney was waiting for it, like a fireman with a net outside a burning building. The safety had committed himself too far and there was no other Viking within waving distance of the tall Cavalier end. Whit was looking over his shoulder tauntingly for the last ten yards of his run to the goal line.

Savage's jaw sagged; then he simply yelled, along with everyone else. George Breck grinned foolishly; Glass had wrapped both arms around Travis and was trying, unsuccessfully, to lift him off the ground.

The noise slackened a little, picked up again as Whitney kicked the seventh point. Savage had to shout into the phone to make himself heard.

"Any more plays you want to put in, Sam, let's have

'em," he burbled. " You want Hearst to carry the ball, just say so."

" Did you ever see a worse-looking pass? " LaCosta exulted. " Like a crippled sea gull. For the love of Mike, don't ever let him try another one, Ed! "

" Why try to beat perfect? I don't want to spoil Junior's record."

That was an exaggeration, of course, but Savage knew that Travis had thrown his last pass of that particular afternoon.

The 7–0 advantage held up through the rest of the first half, and in the second quarter the Cavaliers missed another score by a hand's span, no more. Burnside, obviously shaken by the Hastings touchdown, did not get across mid-field, and the Cavalier sweep series began to move.

But although Burnside gave up a little more ground to the Cavalier wide plays, its line held firm inside the 30, and finally Glass had to go for the long pass. It was just off the finger tips of Tony Corbett in the corner of the end zone. Savage ground a fist into his palm in disappointment.

Still, the Cavaliers came off the field to the accompaniment of cheers, with the confident air of a team in command. Travis, naturally, was the hero of the moment, and the object of waggish comment.

" Did you see Whit waiting for that thing to come down? " Maderas demanded in feigned horror. " He had time to grow a beard."

" You should've taken along something to read, Whit."

"What an arm! Solid glass! "

Then Crump, sitting on the floor with his knees locked between his arms, asked jocularly: " Tell us the truth, Junior. Did you really see Whit, or were you aiming for the stands? "

Travis had responded to the others' gibes with a bland smile and a remark about understandable envy. Now his mouth hardened.

"Turn blue, Vince," he said brusquely. Crump's head jerked up, eyes narrowing.

"Now that's no way to answer a simple question, is it?"

His tone was mild, but Savage recognized the undertone of challenge. He stepped quickly toward Travis.

"What's the difference where he aimed it?" he asked cheerfully. "It went for six."

His eyes and Crump's met for an instant. Then Vince gave a slight shrug and seemed to relax.

"Yeah, it did," he said with indifference. The hush that had enveloped the room during this brief exchange was suddenly dispelled by a dozen voices, but Savage knew that the damage had been done. The sense of squad unity had been torn by this show of undisguised hostility between its best halfback and its best lineman. And Savage admitted to himself that he did not know how to restore the unity.

Yet there was no evidence of disunity in the Cavaliers' play as the second half began. Freeman sprang clear on a fake pass and trap for forty yards down to the Vikings' 25, but again Burnside's granite defense choked off the touchdown thrust.

"Looks as though we have to score from mid-field or no count," Savage said to Breck with a feeble attempt at humor. George shook his head despondently.

"They were waiting for Travis on that one, Ed. Al should have gone off tackle instead of up the middle."

Savage was of the same mind, but refrained from saying so. He saw no profit in second-guessing his own quarterback.

Nor was there any sign of letdown by Hastings as Burn-

94

side, perking up after its successful goal-line stand, began to put together a drive of its own.

The big man was Watkins, handling the ball on three plays out of four, chipping away for three-, four-, and five-yard gains or throwing a short running pass. He seemed tireless and indestructible, bouncing to his feet at once even after being slammed down by the hardest kind of tackle.

As the Hastings rooters implored, " Get that ball! " Burnside moved to the touchdown. Savage, alternately hopeful and gloomy, substituted where he felt he must, and Hastings gave up ground grudgingly. But finally, from the 1-yard line, Watkins hurled himself like a projectile over a mass of bodies on the goal line. Clawson and Crump met him head on at the top of his leap, but not before the ball had been carried across the line momentarily, and that was enough for the score.

Then, for no reason at all, the Burnside place kicker missed the extra point. The Viking line held; he had ample time, but the ball skittered off to the right of the posts as Hastings voices and Savage's spirits rebounded from the depths. Hastings still led, 7–6. One point would be as good as one hundred at the finish, if it held up.

It was one of the longest fifteen minutes in Savage's memory, but one that he watched with a growing pride in his team. Three times in the fourth quarter the Vikings stormed across mid-field, and three times the weary, dogged Cavaliers stopped them.

Clawson broke up the first one with an interception; Bedolla, replacing the tired Whitney at end, halted the second with a fine, smothering rush of Watkins on a crucial third-down play.

Then, with less than two minutes remaining, Burnside reached the Hastings 25, fourth and four. Savage crouched before the bench, throat dry, shirt soaked with perspiration.

Watkins started wide, holding the ball high and threatening the pass if the opening to run wasn't there. He could not find a receiver open, and so he slanted toward the far side line. It was Crump who nailed him at the line of scrimmage, diving low and pinning Watkins' legs in a picture of the perfect tackle. Still grasping the runner's legs tightly, Crump rolled over with him twice, came to his knees, and then dumped him back to the ground like a sack of flour.

It was theatrical, a grandstanding bit, but the ecstatic Savage was not begrudging Crump the gesture. Vince had saved the game; he could turn handsprings if he desired. Savage whirled toward the bench and called excitedly for Kassowitz. So he did not see Watkins, getting up slowly, limp painfully off the field, his arm around the shoulder of the Burnside trainer.

Little more than a minute later, after Kassowitz had run three meaningless but time-consuming quarterback sneaks, the gun sounded. As the joyful Hastings rooters poured down from the stands, a buoyant Savage made his way across the field to meet the losing coach.

～

"Well, Sambo," Savage said affectionately, slinging his coat over a chair, "between you and Vince and maybe a couple of other guys, I look as though I knew something about coaching football. I hope the truth never comes out."

LaCosta snorted derisively and flung himself full length on the sofa. The postgame routine — the individual check on each player, the exchange with old grads and alumni — had required nearly two hours — and the exhilaration of victory was beginning to wear off. Both were tired and looked it.

"Don't try to palm off any credit on me," Sam said. "You know as well as I do that without Crump, we lose by two touchdowns at least."

"That's true." Savage said it with reluctant admiration. "He's the best college guard I've ever seen. But he scares me a little. I thought he was going to go for Travis in the dressing room at half time."

"Yeah. Junior doesn't like him a little bit."

"I wonder why — whether it's something specific, or if they just rub each other the wrong way."

Sam raised himself on one elbow.

"It's specific, Ed. I did a little ear-bending around the lockers today. Joe Scarsella and Travis are close friends. I think Junior blames Vince for Joe's injury."

Savage's eyes clouded.

"That one again," he said wearily. "Sam, I'm no mind reader. Vince has played it straightaway except for that Linfield mess. I have to give him the benefit of the doubt."

"Sure," LaCosta said laconically. "Same as today, with Watkins."

Savage stared uncomprehending for a moment.

"Watkins? Nothing happened to him!"

It was Sam's turn to look surprised.

"Didn't you see him being helped off after Vince nailed him on fourth down when we stopped them the last time?"

Bewildered, Savage said he hadn't.

"Oh." Sam looked nonplused. "And nobody said anything about it? From Burnside, I mean?"

"Not a whisper, Sam."

"O.K., I owe Vince an apology," LaCosta said, sighing. "Except he ain't gonna get it. Ed, I had the glasses on that play, and I thought Crump rolled with him more than

97

he had to. Easy enough to give a guy's leg a little twist when you've got both of 'em wrapped. It's been tried on you, I'll bet."

"But it doesn't add up, Sam! If Vince was trying to get Watkins, why did he wait until the end of the game? The man had already done us all the damage he could."

"I dunno. With a certain type, it's a reflex action. When you've got a guy in the nutcracker, squeeze him even if it doesn't help you a bit. When I saw Watkins limping off, I thought —"

He broke off and gave a quick shake of his head, as though to rid himself of unpleasant doubts.

"I'm wrong, I guess," he said. "Only, for my own peace of mind, I wish Vince hadn't given him that extra flip."

So do I, Sam, Savage thought, the keen edge of the day's triumph suddenly dulled. So do I.

8

LOOK," said Fitzgerald, with the patient air of a man explaining to a backward child, " we beat Kentfield and Western, O.K.? That makes us five and one, so if we beat Mount Royal, then we win it by licking Rossiter, no matter what happens to the other clubs. Suppose Burnside or Linfield dumps either of 'em, we're home free."

Savage, standing just inside the door of the trainer's room, heard the stocky Fitz analyzing the Cavaliers' Rose Bowl chances for Buzz Fairchild, a second-string tackle. Fairchild's reply held a measure of doubt.

" Oh, sure, we'll beat Kentfield. And Western isn't much. But we're no cinch against Mount Royal, Fitz. And Rossiter. I don't know about the Raiders."

"You watch, pal. We'll handle 'em when the time comes."

Their cleats rang on the tiled floor as they moved down the corridor. Savage, smiling faintly, waited until the sound of their voices had faded before he emerged from the trainer's room.

He had had no intention of eavesdropping, but he had been arrested by Fitzgerald's calm assurance that the Cavaliers would defeat their next two foes just as a matter of course. Even the dubious Fairchild had accepted that un-questioningly.

It was, Savage thought, part of the campus reaction to the Burnside game. Not quite the same as that which had followed the victory over Linfield, but a more solidly rooted conviction that after half a dozen dismal seasons, Hastings was actually a contender for the Big Eight championship.

By nature cautious, Savage had pointed out to the ebullient Murchison that the season was only half over.

" I know it, Ed," Cal had responded happily, " but we're not used to being in the running even at the halfway mark. I've listened to coaches explain why they're losing, but you're the first one who keeps apologizing for winning. Why not enjoy it? "

Why not, indeed? Without deluding himself about the strength of his Cavaliers, Savage was now taking a more optimistic view of the future. Not in the matter of games won and lost, he admitted, for next year would be difficult. The heart and muscle of this season's team would go, and Babe Bassich's freshmen were not strong.

But he felt he had laid the foundation for the kind of football team Hastings wanted. Nothing had come from the Burnside camp, from either Dave Patterson, the coach, or unofficial sources, about the injury to Watkins. To Savage, that was sufficient proof that it had been accidental. He had examined the films of the play carefully, but they only showed Crump hitting the Viking runner cleanly and then rolling with him like a tumbler. It wasn't possible to read a man's mind from film, either. Besides, the injury had proved minor, not severe enough to keep Watkins from missing a day's practice.

LaCosta said nothing more on the subject. Like Marty Regan, Savage thought, Sam was seeing things under the bed — at least where Vince was concerned. Savage had no illusions about penetrating Crump's air of cynical detachment; so long as Vince stayed in line, it did not matter.

Nor had he been able to pierce Junior Travis' cool reserve. This disturbed him a little; he had the impression that Junior did not trust him completely.

He was also aware that Breck enjoyed the confidence of most of the veterans who had been brought in by Jim Trainor. If they took their personal problems to anyone on the staff, it was to George, not to him. That was understandable.

But with the rest of the squad, Savage felt that he was making progress slowly toward the relationship he and Sam had known at Niles. There they had served not only as coaches, but as unofficial counselors as well, with whom the players could discuss their affairs off the gridiron — grades, girls, finances. It was as much a part of the job as teaching a man how to block.

So he was in a cheerful frame of mind as he went to the practice field. Remembering his promise to Sarah, he singled out Jerry McLain and was assured that the tardy themes had been turned in.

It was a good practice, and Savage decided to end it with a touch of scrimmage to polish the offense. He called the plays in the first-team huddle, with the seconds aligned in the type of defense Kentfield was expected to use.

The two elevens went at the job spiritedly, and Savage was generally pleased with the execution of the offense. But the first team had trouble running a halfback dip at tackle that developed into a sweep to the outside. Chuck Bedolla, the defensive left end, kept getting in the way, because Hearst wasn't blocking him properly.

Chuck was getting good, Savage told himself with satisfaction, but Hearst was making the end's task easier. After

101

Bedolla had piled up the sweep for the second time, Savage called Larry out of the huddle.

"You're trying to take him the wrong way," he explained patiently. "Hook him inside if he comes in sharp, drive him out if he floats, but in either case, get your body in front of him and keep digging. Like this."

He demonstrated and the tackle nodded, scowling.

"Call that play again," he said. "I'll get him this time."

But he did not, and pounded his fist angrily on the ground before he got up.

"Larry, you made the same mistake again," Savage called impatiently, and saw the boy's face redden.

A few minutes later, he had the offense try the play once more. Bedolla, hand-fighting Hearst cleverly, reached out to trip Travis with one hand as the halfback tried to slide past.

"Nice going, Chuck, nice!" LaCosta crowed. Hearst and Bedolla untangled and rose, and suddenly Hearst swung his right hand and hit Chuck on the jaw, sending him staggering backward.

For an instant, everyone on the field stood frozen as though in a tableau. Then as the dumfounded Savage started forward, Crump and Clawson closed on Hearst. Clawson pinioned his arms while Crump put a hand on his chest and forced him back. Larry made no struggle; from his expression, he was astounded by his own action.

Savage headed for Bedolla, now flanked by LaCosta and Breck. The end was holding his jaw and looked completely dazed.

"What'd he do that for?" he demanded plaintively, with no immediate show of resentment. He shook his head to clear it; then his eyes blazed. "Why, the dirty — "

"Easy, Chuck," Savage said firmly, gripping his arm.

102

" Go on over there and sit down. George, stay with him."

He wheeled and strode toward Hearst, standing dejectedly in a group of players who were exchanging bewildered looks. They fell back to open a path for the coach.

" All right, Larry," he said icily. " Wait on the side lines for me."

He turned to the others.

" All right, let's get back to work. Fairchild, take right tackle. Sam, you run 'em, will you? "

Then he walked slowly toward the solitary figure of Hearst, standing slump-shouldered on the far side of the field. He was the picture of dejection.

" Well, Larry, what prompted that? " Savage's voice was low, but steel-hard. " Was Chuck roughing you up? That the reason? "

" No, nothing like that," Hearst said abjectly. " It was just that he was giving me a bad time on that play and I — I just blew my stack, I guess. I'm awful sorry, Coach, awful sorry."

There was a pleading look in his eyes. Savage, cold with anger, recognized Hearst's sincerity, but he would not accept regret as an excuse. His first impulse was to throw Hearst off the squad, but he fought back the words. Even if that were the only possible solution, it would be wiser to deliver the verdict after he'd cooled off.

" I'm sorry too, Larry. If that's your only reason for slugging a teammate, you'd better call it a day. Come to my office at one o'clock tomorrow and we'll talk about it."

" O.K.," Hearst said miserably. He began to walk toward the gate, then broke into a run, as though fleeing an invisible pursuer. Savage could not restrain a twinge of sympathy. Larry was a fierce competitor, but he had not learned to keep that competitive spirit under control. Savage felt himself at fault in that respect, but he could not let a man off with a mere reprimand for slugging. Not with a team like the Cavaliers.

The earlier zest had gone out of the scrimmage, that was apparent. But Savage kept it going until he judged that Hearst had sufficient time to dress and leave the locker room. He was thankful that, because of the scrimmage, he had kept the gates closed on this practice to all but accredited newspapermen and correspondents, and he had seen none of those. The incident would not be a secret very long, he knew, but he might be spared newspaper questioning until he had reached a decision.

"What are you going to do about Larry?" George Breck asked somberly in the coaches' room.

"Right now, he's off the squad," Savage answered in tired fashion. "I want to think it over. Maybe he won't play any more this season. I just don't know."

"All season?" Breck was aghast. "Isn't that kind of rough? The boy just lost his head; he isn't vicious."

"Rough on Chuck, too," LaCosta observed, unsmiling. "That jaw of his doesn't feel too good."

"I'll make up my mind when I talk to him tomorrow," Savage said. "But nobody gets the green light to go around belting people."

LaCosta made a discreet departure from the house when the two of them came back from training table, a gesture Savage appreciated. Sam knew that it was properly the problem of the head coach, and did not want to intrude, even by his mere presence.

Blast! Savage thought helplessly. He did not want to be too harsh, yet he could not afford to be too lenient. He was still undecided when he went to his office next morning. To his surprise, Bedolla was standing in the corridor, obviously waiting for him.

" Hello, Chuck. Come on in. How's the chin feel? "

The end instinctively raised a hand to an irregular discolored area on his face.

" Not bad," he said diffidently. " Larry's a pretty good hitter."

" I imagine he is," Savage said dryly. Bedolla looked uncertain, as though he did not know how to begin.

" It's about that I wanted to see you, Coach," he began hesitantly. " I was plenty sore at first, but I got to thinking about it, and it was just one of those things. I wouldn't want Larry to get into serious trouble on account of it."

Savage frowned, pondering his reply, and Bedolla, like a man diving into chill waters, went on hurriedly, the words tumbling out.

" Larry came around and apologized last night. He was all broken up about it. I know it won't happen again, Coach."

"At the moment, Larry's not a member of the team, Chuck," Savage said slowly. " You're asking that he be reinstated, then? "

" Well, whatever it comes out." Bedolla was obviously embarrassed. " You're the boss, but I just wanted you to know that I didn't want him punished on account of what he did to me. Anyone could get excited the way he did."

Savage felt himself wavering. In a way, Bedolla was not the only injured party; Larry's action was an offense against every one of his teammates. But Chuck's plea merited consideration.

" I'll think about it, Chuck. I appreciate your coming here. I hope Larry does too."

" Please, Coach," Bedolla said in alarm, " don't tell him. Or anyone else. This is just between us. Please? "

Savage smothered a smile. Funny how kids dreaded to be thanked for a generous gesture.

"Between us," he agreed, and Bedolla departed. Savage made a steeple of his fingers and stared at them in concentration. This was Bedolla's idea alone, he was sure. Chuck was a friend of Junior Travis, a product of the same high school, and Savage guessed that Travis, in the same circumstances, might not have been so quick to forgive.

He made up his mind at that moment. Hearst would have to sweat it out for a while — through the Kentfield game Saturday, or it was no penalty at all. Then he could return, but strictly on his good behavior.

But he did not reveal this to the penitent Hearst when that youth appeared in his office later.

"I'll make it brief, Larry," he said in a stern manner. "I'm not going to lecture you; I know you regret what you did, but I can't overlook it. You're indefinitely suspended from the squad. If you feel like it, see me Monday morning, and we'll talk about it some more. That's all."

Hearst's downcast features brightened momentarily at the invitation to return, but there was no encouragement in Savage's unsmiling countenance. Larry ducked his head and left without a word.

Upon reflection, Savage decided to tell neither Breck nor LaCosta that Hearst's suspension would be lifted the following week. If Breck knew, Savage wasn't sure that the information might not get back to Larry. Yet he did not feel right about informing one of his assistants and not the other, despite the difference in their personal relationships.

Breck took the news with a glum look and a shake of his head. LaCosta, equally serious, said he did not see how Savage could do anything else.

"If one man can yet away with it, why not everyone?" he asked pointedly. Breck said he supposed there was something in that, but it was evident that he did not approve.

Savage had not expected that he would. George was concerned with getting the job done, and he was thinking only of what Hearst's absence would mean against Kentfield and other future foes.

But Savage was frankly jolted by Cal Murchison's reaction. He thought the athletic director should be informed, since Hearst's absence from the traveling squad was certain to evoke questions.

"Suspension? Do you think that's necessary, Ed? After all, it's really just a family matter, and you say the boy's apologized. Why not let it go at that?"

"Cal, this is a matter of principle," Savage protested. "Larry has to play by the rules like everyone else."

"I understand that." Murchison sounded faintly irritated. "It's just that — oh well, you're the coach. Do as you see fit."

He hung up abruptly. Savage wondered unhappily if he really understood Murchison at all.

He made no announcement to the squad, for none was necessary. Hearst was not at practice, Fairchild was running at right tackle; the circumstances were self-explanatory.

Discipline or not, Kentfield was still on the schedule, and after a comparatively subdued meal at the training table, the coaches went back to the strategy room. It was after nine when Savage and LaCosta returned to the house. The telephone was ringing insistently as Savage pushed open the door.

It was Jake Gledhill, not a jovial Jake, but a crisply efficient reporter seeking information.

"I understand you've kicked Larry Hearst off the squad for slugging. Any truth in it?"

"Where'd you get your information, Jake?" Savage sparred.

107

"Well, it doesn't seem to be any state secret, even though I was among the last to know," Jake said edgily. "One of the secretaries here heard it from her kid brother. He picked it up on the campus. And I see Larry's name isn't on the traveling squad. What about it?"

Jake was miffed, no doubt of that.

"I didn't make any announcement of it," Savage said placatingly. "But it's true that Hearst is suspended from the team. For disciplinary reasons."

"The breach of discipline being a punch at Chuck Bedolla?"

The campus grapevine was quite accurate, Savage thought ruefully.

"That's correct, Jake."

"No objections to my printing it, I suppose?" Jake sounded sarcastic.

"I can't tell you what to print, Jake."

"I know you can't. I just wanted to know if you objected." He hung up.

"Trouble?" LaCosta asked gently.

"How to make friends," Savage said with a note of bitterness. "Jake is sore because I didn't tell him as soon as it happened. Cal thinks I should have simply overlooked the whole thing. You got any opinions?"

"Yeah, that I do." LaCosta flashed one of his rare grins. "My opinion is that we should take care of Kentfield and let Cal and Jake argue with each other. There's only one way to play this particular hand and you're doing it, Ed."

"Thank you for those kind words, Samuel J. LaCosta," Savage said with mock formality. "They may be the last I'll ever hear."

As it turned out, his jest was not far wide of the mark.

9

THE Kentfield airport was crowded, and it was pure chance that Savage, crossing the waiting room in the wake of the Cavalier squad, caught a glimpse of the big man at the newsstand. He veered in that direction and came up behind Marty Regan just as he turned.

"Hi, Marty."

"Hello, Ed." Regan smiled, shifting a bulging brief case to extend a hand in greeting. "I knew you were coming in, but I didn't know the exact time."

"You're here for the game?"

"No, as a matter of fact. I'm on my way home — go out in twenty minutes. I had some personal business down here, but my team's playing tonight, so I have to get back."

"Oh." Savage felt a twinge of disappointment. "Have you seen us this season?"

"Yes, last week against Burnside. You've done very well, Ed. My congratulations."

"Thanks." Savage's disappointment deepened. So Marty had been on the campus and had not come around to say hello. "I wonder if you've changed your mind since the last time we talked."

Regan said unhappily: "I'll be frank. No, from what I hear."

" From what you hear! " Savage could not keep the bitterness out of his voice. " You saw the Burnside game. Anything wrong with that one? "

Regan said softly, " Dave Patterson thought so."

At the mention of the Burnside coach, Savage bristled. " That's the first I've heard of it. What was wrong with it — besides his losing? "

" If you knew Dave better, you wouldn't have said that, Ed." Regan was patient, but reproving. " If he had won, he might have complained. But because he lost, he won't say anything publicly. Watkins told him his leg was twisted on purpose, and Dave advised him to forget it. But he believes the kid."

" You do too, I suppose."

" I don't know him," Regan said, shrugging. "Is it so farfetched, Ed? You set down a player this week for slugging one of his own men, or so I read."

Savage flushed. It wasn't fair for Marty, starting from a mistaken assumption, to add to it these isolated incidents, and come up with an answer that was wrong, entirely wrong.

" What you read about Larry Hearst was correct," he said stiffly. " He got excited. I suspended him. It's happened on other teams, you know."

" Look, Ed, you're not answerable to me for anything." Marty sounded impatient now. " I don't enjoy hacking this around, so why don't we drop it overboard? Anyway, I hope you win 'em all, sincerely. Now I'd better get on that plane."

" O.K., Marty. Give my best to Isabelle."

Regan nodded and moved toward the gates. Savage watched his retreating figure with a sense of growing frustration, then went outside to the waiting bus.

" Wasn't that Marty Regan you were talking to? " Breck

asked. Savage said noncommittally that it was, and Breck remarked that Regan had sent some good boys to Hastings.

" Nobody in the last couple of years, though," he added reflectively. " I don't think he liked Jim, but with you and him being old teammates, we ought to have a better chance. This Henderson now — I hear he's something."

Is George being subtle, Savage wondered, or is he actually unaware of Marty's attitude? He knew of Henderson, a tackle at Proctor Central, but not from Regan. Other Hastings alumni had sounded out the boy, found him unenthusiastic.

" I don't think we have much chance to get Henderson," he said. " Burnside seems to be his choice."

Breck said, " Oh? " and lapsed into silence. Savage stared moodily out the window as the bus snaked through the heavy evening traffic. There was a sizable Hastings alumni group in the Kentfield area, and he was to address them that evening. Cal Murchison, unable to make this trip, had arranged the meeting. Additionally, there were several high school coaches with whom Savage had appointments. Out of it all, Hastings might get a player or two. It was going to need them, after this year's crop had graduated.

~

If there was a low pressure game on the Cavalier schedule, Kentfield qualified. It was the only non-Conference opponent Hastings played this season, and since it was not a member of the Big Eight, the game did not count in the standings. Furthermore, the Bulldogs had a young team that had won only one game so far. They ran from a semi-spread formation and passed a lot, but defensively they were not strong. Savage thought the Cavaliers could run against them.

His confidence was justified from the very first play, as

Freeman turned the Kentfield left end on a pitchout and scurried thirty-two yards past mid-field. The drive to the touchdown was uninterrupted as Glass, mixing plays adroitly, alternated sweeps and slants off the guards down to the 5-yard line.

From there, Travis followed the blocking of Crump and Clawson into the end zone, Whitney kicked, and it was 7–0 with only six minutes gone.

Although he had anticipated some measure of success, Savage was frankly surprised at the ease with which the Cavaliers had moved, and said as much to Breck.

" Looks like they'll never handle that pitchout," George agreed happily.

The Bulldogs were no more effective on offense. The semispread offered little running threat up the middle, so Hastings' defense was concentrated on the receivers, with results highly gratifying to the Cavalier coaches. The Bulldogs completed only one short swing pass to a flanker back before they had to kick.

Glass caught the punt on the run, like an outfielder going after a sinking line drive. He was immediately knocked head over heels by a Bulldog end, but held on to the ball.

" Jupiter! " Savage had burst out in alarmed protest as he saw that the quarterback was going to try the difficult catch.

" I hope he doesn't try *that* again," Breck said dryly as the quarterback bounced jauntily to his feet.

" Brother-r-r! " Savage's relief mingled with admiration. Nine out of ten safety men would have let that low twisting kick hit and roll rather than risk the fumble. So he had cured Glass of being gun-shy on punts. Now he had to start curbing his audacity. It was a strange business.

The Cavaliers drove to another touchdown at once, Glass

112

himself going the last eight yards on a keeper play, freezing a heavy-footed defender with a neat change of pace. Whitney made it 14–0, and Savage thought it time to give his quarterback a breather.

Glass came off wearing a cocky grin.

"We've got these guys wrapped for mailing, Coach," he said in airy fashion. "Did you see me give that halfback the in-and-out just now? He's still looking for his shoes."

Savage assumed an expression of severity.

"I saw it. I also saw you making like Willie Mays with that punt. That one had 'fumble' written all over it."

"I hung on to it, didn't I?" Glass asked, looking so crestfallen that Savage could not maintain a straight face.

"O.K., Al, you did that," he chuckled, throwing an arm across the quarterback's shoulders. "But please, either let that kind roll or make the catch look easier. You're making an old man of me. Now sit down and take it easy."

Kentfield made a faint stir at the start of the second period as Fairchild got himself trapped and the Bulldog tailback ran the short side for good yardage. But Crump shot the gap the next time to nail the runner for six lost, and the threat petered out.

The second-team backfield, working behind most of the regular line, ran it to 20–0 at the half. A high pass from center spoiled the try for point, but that did not disturb Savage as much as the fact that Tony Corbett had picked up a painful Charley horse.

The right half was hobbling around the dressing room, and it was evident he would play no more that afternoon. That meant Jerry McLain or Steve Spicer would have to replace him, and neither was particularly sharp on pass defense. Obviously, Kentfield was going to throw a lot; there was little else it could do when it was 20 points down.

But Kentfield did not score in the third period, and neither did Hastings, although the Cavaliers' second team ran up considerable yardage.

It was rather a frustrating session for Savage, although he was not worried about the outcome. A fumble by Clampett halted one thrust; another went awry when Fitzgerald missed a starting signal and jumped off side.

Breck exclaimed disgustedly at this and Savage echoed his disapproval. The sloppy execution annoyed him, even though there was no pressing need for another touchdown.

Still, with that many opportunities, it was irritating not to capitalize on at least one of them, particularly since LaCosta kept pointing out obvious holes in the Bulldog defense.

So when McLain returned a Kentfield punt to the home team's 34-yard line early in the fourth period, Savage sent his regulars in for the first time since the intermission.

"The hook pass should go," he told Glass. "Their left line backer is doing a lot of red-dogging."

It worked fine, first rattle, with Maderas jumping across the line and then turning to take the throw, but the play was called back because a Cavalier was detected using hands illegally.

"Oh, for the love of Mike!" Savage exclaimed. "Did you see who that call was on, George?"

Breck said he couldn't tell, but Vince Crump was talking to the umpire, and that official was shaking his head and making a gesture with his arm and elbow.

Of course, it had to be Vince, Savage thought wrathfully. What could he say to him? "Don't do it again," was about the limit.

The penalty was just enough to end the chance to score, although it was close. Travis got part of the fifteen yards back, and a jump pass to Whitney added some more, but

114

on fourth down Glass slipped as he tried to cut through a huge hole at tackle. When the sticks were brought out for measurement, the Cavaliers were a foot short.

Well, we don't need it, Savage thought resignedly. There were only eight minutes left to play, and there was no point in leaving any of his first stringers in there to run the risk of being racked up. He turned toward the bench.

As Crump came to the side line, Savage met him with a query about the penalty. Vince stared at him.

" Yeah, it was on me," he said curtly. " That ump has corners on his head. Said I had my hands out too far. I didn't."

It was a simple statement, with no hint of apology or regret. But some sort of admonition was required, and Savage was on the verge of making it when his attention was diverted by the sight of a gold-jerseyed Kentfield end streaking along in front of the Hastings bench. He was a good three yards in front of the panting, straining Spicer. The receiver had got behind him, and although Kassowitz was closing in at an angle, Savage saw that neither was going to get there in time if the pass were truly thrown.

It was. The Bulldog end took it over his shoulder and drew away from the agonized pursuit of the Hastings pair. He ran like a sprinter; Savage realized that he had just entered the game and that the Kentfield passer too was new. He could obviously throw the ball a mile. The Cavalier regulars weren't going to get that additional rest, after all.

Crump was still standing beside him.

" Better go back in there, Vince," Savage said, and turned to look for the rest of his first string.

Crump gave a sardonic laugh.

" I can't. I've had it for today. Remember? "

With sudden dismay, Savage realized that was true. Not

only Vince, but every other Cavalier regular whom he had sent in earlier in the quarter and then taken out again was prevented from returning. The substitution rule provided that only players who had started a period could leave and come back during that period. The second team had been on the field when the quarter began.

"That's right," Savage said, as though it were merely an oversight of no great importance. Inwardly he berated himself for his hurried, unthinking carelessness, and cast an apprehensive glance at the scoreboard clock.

There were only seven minutes remaining, and even though there were some inexperienced hands on the field, Kentfield couldn't score twice in that time.

He relaxed a little as the Bulldog try for point sailed wide of the goal posts to leave it 20–6.

"Looks like I pulled a skull," he confessed sheepishly to Breck, and explained what had happened.

"Gosh, I didn't notice that either," the assistant said anxiously. "Good thing there isn't much time left."

But very quickly it seemed like quite a long time.

Kentfield came up with an ancient stratagem, the onside kick. The kicker swung his foot mightily, then nudged the ball lightly toward the side line.

Buzz Fairchild was the end man in the Hastings front rank, and he was closest to the ball as it trickled across the 50-yard line. That made it anybody's ball, but all Fairchild had to do was fall on it. He did, and it squirted out from under him like a watermelon seed. There was a tangle of arms and legs as players dived for it, and Savage's heart dropped as a gold-jerseyed Bulldog began to clap his hands over his head in a joyful gesture. Kentfield had recovered.

What next? Savage thought in bafflement. The Cavaliers had not been surprised by the old device; Fairchild had been there, but Fairchild had fumbled. Those things happened.

"All right, let's settle down!" he shouted through cupped hands. There was no need to hit the panic button; it was still Hastings' game. But he had better get Spicer out of there. McLain was erratic on pass defense, but he was swift, and Kentfield was going to throw long again to that speedy end, sure as taxes.

Before he could give his hurried instructions to McLain, though, the new Kentfield tailback, Simpkins, was hurling another long, arching pass downfield and a wild shriek went up from the Bulldog rooters. But it was thrown too far, and the end missed the diving catch by inches.

"O.K., Jerry, move," Savage said hoarsely. The palms of his hands were damp.

Spicer came out with dejection in the slump of his shoulders, but Savage gave him a consoling "Good trying, Steve," as the youth went past him. It wasn't Spicer's fault that he couldn't run as fast as the end. Savage knew the blame was his own, for boxing himself into a corner on the substitution rule.

Again Simpkins rolled out to pass, but found no one open. So he began to run, picking up blockers on the way. Fitzgerald had a shot at him near the line of scrimmage, but the runner twisted out of his clutch and went down to the Cavalier 30 before McLain hooked him.

"Come on, Fitz, let's get with it!" Breck yelled angrily. "Should've had him 'way back there."

Crump would have nailed him, Savage thought. But Crump was standing on the side line.

The Bulldogs were on fire now, and the Cavaliers were shaken and uncertain. Murdock, the second-string center, was roaming behind the line, threatening and exhorting, but there was a desperate quality to his shrill voice.

117

Simpkins shot the flare-out pass to his wingback, and McLain knocked the receiver down at once. Still, it gained eight yards, and then Simpkins ran inside tackle for the first down.

The clocked ticked on inexorably. Simpkins could not afford the short gains; it had to be all or nothing. He ran to his right, faked a pass, started to run, then stopped and sent a long, arching aerial into a corner of the end zone.

The Cavaliers had it covered. Kassowitz was there and so was Clampett, and the two of them went up as one with the Kentfield halfback. But the Bulldog was the tallest of the three, and it was he who had the ball when they came down.

Savage wheeled, looking despairingly at the bench as Simpkins booted the extra point to make it 20–13. His eyes searched for someone whose presence might steady the team in these last few minutes. Glass could do it, but Glass couldn't be used. Frederickson, the number three quarterback, was patently too jittery, even as an onlooker, to be of any use at this stage. The best team Hastings could muster was on the field now.

" Let's hang on to that ball! " he shouted. " Watch for that onside kick! "

Kentfield did not try it this time, preferring to gamble on kicking deep and then holding the Cavaliers for three downs. With four minutes remaining, they would still have time to get possession again and throw the long pass. If they could hold.

The kick did go deep, and although McLain had a rolling start up the field, a Bulldog knifed through the blockers and cut him down with an ankle tackle on the 22.

Kassowitz took his time in the huddle, using every second he could without incurring a penalty for delay.

Just one first down, just one, Savage thought imploringly. Kentfield wouldn't lay hands on the ball again if Kas could do that.

The Bulldog stands were screaming, "Fee, fi, fo, fumble!" as Kassowitz sent McLain on the sweep and then tried to go off tackle on a keeper. But Kentfield, sure that Hastings would not risk a pass, stacked an eight-man line against them, and the two plays gained only three yards.

Still, even if the Cavaliers had to kick, Kentfield would have more than half the field to cover in a matter of seconds.

Kassowitz knelt in the huddle, then straightened up, looked at the clock, and bent down again.

Slowly the Cavaliers came up to the line. Kassowitz, his stubby legs churning, came out wide to the right on the option play, his arm cocked to pass. Savage sucked in his breath in apprehension. Surely Kas was not going to throw in this situation!

He did, and hurriedly, as two Kentfield linemen rushed him fiercely. His target was McLain, cutting shallow toward the side line. There was no defender within five yards of him, and had the ball missed him entirely, no harm would have resulted.

But Kassowitz, in his haste, threw behind McLain, who turned and made a fine try for the catch. His fingers reached the ball, just enough to deflect it straight into the hands of the surprised Simpkins, racing over to cover the receiver.

Simpkins took off like a rocket, then swerved back toward the middle of the field, whirling and twisting until Kassowitz finally dragged him down just five yards from the goal line.

Breck's thin face was suffused with rage.

"How could he call that? How could he? Tell me how!"

119

Savage shook his head wordlessly. His throat was dry. If he could lay hands on Kas at the moment, he'd — No, he thought unhappily, he could only console the boy. If the play had worked, the victory would have been nailed down.

Maybe it still could be preserved; maybe the Cavaliers could hold. But even as he offered the silent wish, Simpkins was slamming down to the 1 behind a blocking surge that obliterated Fairchild and Fitzgerald, and he was over on the next play. As the fearful noise from the stands subsided briefly, Simpkins calmly kicked the tying point, and it began again.

Happy enough with the 20–20 score, Kentfield disdained the onside kick, sent the ball deep. Clampett could get back only to the 18-yard line. There was less than a minute of play remaining, and Savage sent in Frederickson with orders to use it up on quarterback sneaks. Even if Freddie only took the ball from center and fell down, that would do.

Kassowitz left the field head down, the walking picture of misery. He went to the side lines near the goal line, not coming directly to the bench, but Savage walked down to meet him.

"Bad break, Kas," he said sympathetically and clapped him lightly on the back. The quarterback looked at him mournfully.

"They were rushing eight, nine men," he said in a contrite manner. "I wanted that first down. Of all the dumb luck! "

"I might have made the same call myself," Savage said, with something less than truth. He did not want to demolish Kas's confidence, already badly shaken. The kid had the makings of a good quarterback.

The gun sounded and Savage braced himself for the

post-mortems. In many respects, the outcome was more depressing than a defeat.

"Well, we didn't get licked," he heard Bedolla say with forced cheerfulness, and Clawson snorted in disgust.

"A tie! That's about as satisfactory as kissing your sister."

The players were lower in spirit than Savage had ever seen them. It was a strange thing about tie games; the triumph rested with the team that scored last.

He did what he could to dispel the gloom.

"All right, fellows," he announced, "you won this game today, and I gave it back to Kentfield. I made a stupid mistake, so don't blame anyone else."

This was greeted by an embarrassing silence, then the low tones of conversation resumed. Mahoney said something out of the side of his mouth to Crump and the guard lifted his shoulders in a gesture which said plainly, "What can you do with a coach like this?"

As Savage anticipated, the reporters were eager to get at him. Even Jake Gledhill seemed to take a grim delight in the examination. Why had he kept the first team on the bench?

"I made a bonehead move," Savage said frankly. "I took them out and couldn't get them back in. But even with my mistakes, we would have won except for a fumble and a freak interception."

"How about that pass?" a Kentfield scribe asked with a sly grin. "That was a bonehead move too, wasn't it?"

"No," Savage said quickly. "I'll take full responsibility for any call by my quarterbacks. The way Kentfield was hitting on those long passes — we wanted to keep the ball at all costs. Kassowitz' idea was fine, even if the execution was faulty. Ordinarily, it's a safe pass even if it misses. As I said, it was a freak interception."

121

Gledhill pulled his glasses down and peered at him.

"How about Hearst? He would have helped today, wouldn't he?"

"Certainly. But I was satisfied with Fairchild's play."

This, too, was only partly true; Fairchild had hurt them. He braced himself for Jake's next question, but the reporter merely grunted, and eventually they let him go.

It was a funny business, he reflected ruefully. One day a coach was a hero, a leader of men; the next day he was a fumbling incompetent — a bum. This was his day to be a bum.

10

THE trip back was a quiet one, and the team plane was met by only a few students, friends of the players. There was no sign of a cheerleader, and Sam LaCosta took note of it.

"If it had been us that scored in the last minute to tie it, the place would have been jammed," he observed. "Shucks, I don't even see Murchison."

"Oh, come on, Sam," Savage said good-humoredly. "You know Cal is busy these days. We'll hear from him."

The first to telephone, however, was Sarah Fleming.

"Oh, Ed, I'm sorry about yesterday. Or should I be? I don't know. After all, you didn't lose the game."

Savage, warmed by the sound of her voice, said lightly: "In this case, it's even worse. We had it won until your Uncle Edward got too smart for his brains. The team is better than the coach."

Sarah said briskly that she was prepared to argue *that* point, and then her tone became serious.

"I know you're terribly busy these days, Ed, but could I see you for a few minutes tomorrow? I'd like to discuss something with you."

"Of course. Why not discuss it now?"

" No-o. Not on the phone. It's really nothing vital. Just —
just interesting."

It was unlike Sarah to be mysterious, and Savage felt a
vague uneasiness. He would have liked to see her at once,
but Babe Bassich was flying back from scouting the Western game, and there simply wasn't time. They agreed to
meet in her office in the English building next morning.

LaCosta, who had discreetly disappeared into his own
room upon learning the identity of the caller, now re-
appeared.

" What time is Babe due? " he inquired.

" Three thirty, if the plane's on time."

But Savage sensed that there was something on Sam's
mind.

" Ed, are you going to do anything about Hearst? "

So that was it. Savage sighed inwardly. He guessed that
Sam's uncompromising point of view and his own were not
going to mesh on this.

" I'm letting him come back tomorrow, Sam. If anything like the Bedolla thing happens again, though, he
goes for keeps. I'll make that clear."

" Oh." LaCosta spoke the single syllable with an inflection that impelled Savage to elaborate.

" I decided that Friday, Sam. I haven't told anyone yet."

Sam said heavily: " I'll speak my piece and then shut up.
I think it's a mistake. First, the penalty isn't stiff enough.
I don't think Larry's really vicious, but he ought to be
kept on ice longer than a week. Second, a lot of people
will think you're reinstating him because Fairchild looked
bad yesterday. I'm not one of them, but that's how it will
look."

Savage said grimly: " What people think isn't going to
affect my decision on this. I'm doing what I believe is fair
to the boy."

LaCosta regarded him quizzically, then permitted himself a faint smile.

"I believe that, too, even though I don't approve. Well, I just wanted to get on the record."

"For the record, Sam," Savage assented gravely. Sam was a man of his word. He would not mention the subject again.

Hearst came to see Savage the next morning, not particularly hopeful. His face lighted up when he heard the verdict.

"Thanks, Coach," he stammered. "You won't be sorry, I promise you."

"I'd better not be, Larry, or you'll never play for Hastings as long as I'm in charge."

Hearst knew he meant it, but it did not dampen Larry's enthusiasm as he lunged, rather than walked, out of the office. Savage did not think he would have to discipline the big tackle again.

He looked at his watch. Time to keep his appointment with Sarah. He had thought about it with increasing disquiet, wondering what it could be that she was reluctant to discuss over the phone.

As he came out into the corridor, he almost collided with Vince Crump.

"Hello, Coach. Got a minute?"

"Sure, Vince," Savage said, inwardly wary. The guard had never before sought him out off the field. "What's on your mind?"

"Well, it's like this," Crump said, his dark eyes fixed on Savage. "Some of us have talked it over and we'd like to see Larry Hearst come back."

"So?" Savage masked his quick interest.

"Of course, we realize he shouldn't have swung on Chuck," Vince went on, with a little deprecatory gesture.

125

"But you know how kids are, Coach. Particularly one like Larry, who's always trying to do his best, even in practice. They get excited. That's what he did, but he's learned his lesson. The fellows feel it would be a good thing for him and the team too if that suspension was lifted."

Crump spoke in a casual man-to-man fashion, two older heads talking about a wayward youngster. Savage found it infuriating, but he did not show it. By itself, the request was eminently reasonable.

"What do you mean exactly when you say ' good for the team '? "

Vince's eyelids drooped slightly and he gave Savage an amused look that implied a wisdom shared between them.

"I don't want to put the rap on anyone," he replied almost apologetically. "But every team wants to win, particularly one that has a chance for the championship. There's the feeling that if Larry had been in there Saturday, we would have won anyway."

The significance of that "anyway" was not lost on Savage. Even if the coach hadn't idiotically painted himself into a corner, Vince was hinting.

"I'm sure Larry would appreciate your intercession," he said evenly. "However, it wasn't necessary. I've already told him to report for practice today. With the understanding, of course, that this is his last chance."

Crump's heavy brows went up. He was obviously unprepared for the answer. Then he showed his fine teeth in a broad smile.

"Why, that's great, Coach," he exclaimed, unable to conceal the triumph in his voice. "Simply great. The fellows'll be glad to hear it."

He wheeled and strode jauntily down the hall, leaving Savage smarting in frustration. Had there been a veiled threat behind Crump's outwardly respectful plea? What would have followed had Savage been in a position to refuse it?

He was still brooding about it when he reached the English building. Sarah Fleming, poring over a pile of papers, gave him a welcoming smile and motioned him to a chair beside her desk.

"Now, doll, what about this mystery that won't stand airing on the telephone?" he asked with a frown. "Am I here in my role as coach or merely as Ed Savage, the well-know human being?"

There was a look of troubled uncertainty on her small oval face.

"A little of both, Ed. Perhaps I've exaggerated its importance. It's about Jerry McLain."

"Jerry?" He straightened in the chair. "He told me last week he'd made up all his work and handed it in."

"He did." Sarah pulled open a drawer, extracted a thin sheaf of papers, and laid them on the desk. "There they are."

"You mean they're not good enough?" Savage was puzzled. That would be a disappointment, but it would hardly necessitate this private conference.

"No," Sarah said unhappily. "They're too good, that's the trouble. I recognized one of them. It had been turned in to me once before — by another student three years ago. I imagine the other two are A papers from another English 2 class of years back. Either that, or Jerry learned to write excellent prose in five days."

There was mute appeal in her eyes.

"Good grief!" Savage said in a tired voice. "That stuff. I wouldn't have thought it of Jerry."

It was an ancient practice, he knew. There were always present on the campus bright boys with a minimum of scruples who would write a theme or an essay for a fee. And in the fraternity houses, those papers that had earned a good grade were often kept in cold storage, so to speak, and passed on or sold to brothers in trouble. But usually the recipient was careful to alter the language somewhat and doubly careful never to submit it twice to the same instructor.

Among other things, McLain had been guilty of extreme negligence.

"What have you done about it, Sarah?"

"Nothing, yet." She made a little fluttering motion with her hands. "I wanted to ask your advice."

"Why, handle it exactly as you would any other case like it, naturally," Savage said with some surprise.

She hesitated.

"You know, it's really the same as cheating, Ed. If I reported it, he'd go up before Student Council."

His expression showed that he had overlooked that aspect of it. Student Council could suspend, even expel, for cheating. Jerry was a bright youth who made good grades in his other subjects, but irresponsible and just lazy enough to try something like this.

"Since you've asked my advice," he said carefully, "I'm suggesting that you don't turn him in to Council. I really don't believe Jerry's fundamentally dishonest. He probably thought he was just being clever. If he's thrown out of school, he'd carry that black mark the rest of his life."

Sarah looked thoughtful.

"I've always thought branding someone a cheater was harsh, even if it was true. I'm glad you agree. But I do have to report him to the dean, Ed. He's flunking the course."

"Certainly you do. What else?" Savage said in wonderment.

"Well, that means he can't play football," Sarah said, eying him dubiously.

With a feeling of shock, Savage understood. This girl, who he thought knew him better than most people, was not sure how far he would go to protect one of his players. She was not even sure, he realized, that he would not ask her, as a favor, to cover up entirely for McLain.

Anger flared in him for an instant, then subsided. If Sarah had doubts, they had sprung only from his actions. Even Sam LaCosta, who knew him best of all, was questioning his real motives for retaining Vince Crump, reinstating Larry Hearst. From the outside, he looked like a man bent on winning.

"There are no special rules for footballers, Sarah," he said softly after a moment. "I thought you knew that."

She seemed confused and slightly embarrassed.

"Of course, Ed. I — I just thought you'd want to know about Jerry. Rather than hear it from some other source."

"I appreciate it. Would you like me to break it to him? I want to talk to him about it anyway."

"Oh, would you?" she exclaimed gratefully. "I know it's my responsibility, but I really dread it."

"Leave it to me," he said gently. "And thanks. I think the boy has enough good stuff to be worth the trouble."

If it was there, he was going to shake it out of McLain.

He intercepted Jerry as he came whistling into the gym before practice, and put it to him in blunt terms.

Panic showed for an instant in the halfback's face, then vanished as he maintained heatedly that the themes were his own handiwork and no one else's.

"They are?" There was an ominous quality in Savage's

voice. "Miss Fleming doesn't think so. She could turn you in to Council, but she won't. She'll just give you a big fat zero on those three papers and you'll go on probation.

"I admit that would be unjust if you really did write them, and you could go to the head of the English department and protest. But then you might have to demonstrate how well you can write, and if it didn't convince the professor, then you'd be up for Council for sure."

McLain's face had gone fiery red as Savage spoke, and he wet his lips nervously.

"O.K., so I didn't write them," he muttered sullenly. "Lots of others have done it, I bet. And not just athletes, either."

"That's a stupid attitude, Jerry, and you're not stupid. A fellow with your intelligence ought to make the most of his chances, and you want to throw all of them away because you think the rules are for somebody else, not you. How would you feel — how would your parents feel — if you were expelled for this? It's happened, you know."

McLain's defiance had oozed away; he looked frightened.

"What am I supposed to do, then?"

"Go to work, man," Savage said impatiently. "You'll go on probation, naturally, and that means no more football. You could use the extra time to make up your work. If you flunk English 2, you'll roll, probably; even if you don't roll, you'll have to repeat it next term. Why not beat that rap? If you give it an honest try and still have difficulty, come to see me. I'll be glad to help."

"You mean help me with themes?" McLain asked incredulously.

"Sure. I'm not setting up as a tutor, but I did pass English 2. Besides, it's purely selfish on my part. I'd like to count on you for next year."

Jerry managed a weak grin.

"Well, sure, Coach. I — I'll do my best. And thanks."

"Don't thank me." Savage was curt. "Thank Miss Fleming for giving you a chance to come out of this clean."

As the subdued youth turned to go, Savage said: "Just one more thing, Jerry. If you had to pay anyone for those themes, demand your money back."

McLain looked baffled for a moment, then smiled uncertainly. Savage watched him go with a speculative frown. Maybe he was letting Jerry off the hook too lightly. But if Larry Hearst warranted a second opportunity, why not McLain? A man couldn't pass absolute final judgment on kids like that for a first offense.

The tall, spare figure of Cal Murchison lay in wait for him at the practice field.

"Sorry I couldn't make the plane yesterday," Cal said briskly. "I was all tied up with the Athletic Board. How did that alumni meeting go Friday night?"

Savage summarized it briefly.

"We have a lot of spadework to do there, Ed." Murchison showed some concern. "I'll be frank — one or two of the Board members think we've lost too much ground with our own alumni. They wonder if we're doing a proper selling job in the high schools."

Savage became aware that he had a headache.

"'You have to make calls if you want to make sales,'" he quoted the maxim ruefully. "We don't have too much time during the season."

"Of course you don't. This isn't meant as criticism, Ed. All of us are very much pleased by the team's showing. Though I must admit I was disappointed when we lost that big lead Saturday. I thought we had that one in our hip pocket."

He looked at Savage questioningly.

"As I told the team, it was my fault, Cal. I got my feet crossed and tossed it away."

Murchison was sympathetic.

"Easy enough to get mixed up. The way they change the rules every year, it's a miracle that anyone understands them. Besides, it wasn't a Conference game; we've still got a good chance."

"Larry Hearst is back on the squad, Cal. But we're losing Jerry McLain. He's in trouble with his grades."

"Hearst back?" The athletic director's face lighted up. "I think that's a good move, Ed. I'm sorry about McLain, though you don't really need him this year, do you?"

"I didn't put Larry back because I needed him, Cal. I think he's worth another try, that's all."

Murchison gave him a puzzled look.

"I didn't mean to imply you did," he said quickly. "But he will be a help."

That was how it looked, Savage thought — a matter of expediencey. He was not surprised that Jake Gledhill took the same point of view.

The sports writer called him that evening.

"Well, I see you've pardoned Hearst," he said with a hint of sarcasm.

"I think he's learned his lesson." Savage pretended to ignore the gibe.

"Looks like you did too. Such as that he's a better tackle than Fairchild. Was it your own decision, or were you asked to put him back?"

Savage tightened like a bow drawn taut.

"What do you mean by that?" he demanded. "No one tells me who to play, get that straight."

Jake's voice was unruffled.

"I didn't say that. But were you asked? By some of the players, for instance?"

132

So that was it, Savage thought bitterly. He was positive that Chuck Bedolla hadn't talked. It could only be Crump or one of the "fellows" he had represented. And Crump or one of them had let it be known that the coach had been approached, and Hearst was back, wasn't he?

"Yes, I was asked, Jake," he said. "That had no bearing on my decision."

He didn't think Gledhill believed him.

"In case you haven't heard," he added, "we've lost a halfback — Jerry McLain. Scholastic trouble. I couldn't reinstate *him* even if I wanted to."

"No, I hadn't heard. McLain, eh? Well, with Travis and Clampett, you can spare him."

Savage imagined how Gledhill looked as he wrote down that piece of information. A cynical glint in his eye, undoubtedly. He had lost an advocate and gained a critic, and he regretted it, but he would not waste time in regret. His first responsibility was to Hastings, and that responsibility included beating Western on Saturday. For the second straight week, the Cavaliers had to travel, but then they caught the two big ones, Mount Royal and Rossiter, at home, and Savage liked that part of the scheduling.

Whether the team was smarting over Kentfield's undeserved tie, or whether Hearst's return made a real difference, he could not determine. But the fact remained that the Cavaliers beat Western rather handily, 27–7.

Savage went in with the honest conviction that Hastings could win if the breaks were even. He could not have predicted that the Cavaliers' ferocious defensive pressure would cause Western to fumble three times in the first twenty minutes and force two hurried passes that were intercepted.

Glass did not waste any opportunities. He scored the first touchdown himself after Casper had retrieved a Pioneer bobble on the home team's 12-yard line. He fooled the defense and Savage, too, on the next play, faking so cleverly to Freeman up the middle that Savage was still watching the fullback as Al sprinted into the end zone with the ball.

Then Hearst partially blocked a punt, deflecting it into a puny ten-yard kick fluttering out of bounds, and Junior Travis alternated with Freeman in bucking to the score on six plays.

Western mounted one thrust, but was halted short of the Cavalier 30, and Hastings went in to the dressing room at half time with a 13–0 lead.

Savage reminded the squad that a week ago they were in front by 20–0.

" This is a tougher outfield than Kentfield," he warned. " Let's not start coasting."

"We're tougher than we were last Saturday," Crump said, grinning, and flung an arm across Hearst's shoulders. " Did you see the lad tearing up the turf out there? "

Hearst ducked his head in embarrassment.

" Aw, cut it out, Big Dog," he muttered. Vince winked at Savage in knowing fashion.

The Cavaliers did not let down. Western fought it out stubbornly, closing to 13–7 on a series of short passes, and Savage unconsciously quickened his nervous striding up and down in front of the bench.

But Freeman took the kickoff on the goal line, darted up the center until he saw a tunnel at the 25, slanted into it, and came out in the clear at mid-field. A Pioneer over-hauled him on the 9, but Hastings was not going to be denied after a ninety-yard run, and Travis went over on the third play.

That broke the home team's back and it never threat-ened seriously again. To Savage's great satisfaction, Kassowitz directed the Cavaliers' final touchdown on a sustained march, calling the plays with confidence and assurance. There was no indication that last week's unfortunate experience had undermined the boy's self-reliance.

It's like a pilot walking away from a crash, Savage thought. If he didn't go right up again, his usefulness could be destroyed.

Just before the finish, as some of the fans were beginning to depart, the loud-speaker blared the information that Mount Royal had upset Rossiter.

The Cavalier bench reacted as though Hastings had just scored again. They were in a three-way tie with the two big ones.

" What do you know? " Savage said wonderingly to the elated Breck. " I'll be interested in learning how that happened."

" We're in business, Ed," George said joyfully. " We'll catch that Pasadena special yet."

The Rose Bowl, Savage thought. Breck was right; it was possible now. He had never really thought so, even in his most optimistic frame of mind after Hastings' early season successes. He knew what he had, and he thought he knew what the Hurricanes and the Raiders had, and he could not honestly visualize the Cavaliers beating either. Impossible? No, just highly unlikely.

If we were awfully lucky . . . The thought made him a little lightheaded, and he tried to put it away. But it remained, and the boundless enthusiasm the Mount Royal victory had created among the players could not be restrained.

None was more enthusiastic than Cal Murchison. He burst into the dressing room, eyes alight, and descended upon Savage.

" How did you like that Rossiter score? " he demanded,

as excited as a freshman rooter. "Man, there won't be room in our stadium next Saturday for everyone who wants to see that game. And we're going to win it, too."

"I'm for that, Cal," Savage said dryly. "Now if the Hurricanes will only co-operate —"

"We'll co-operate 'em! The way that defense played today!" He lowered his voice. "That Hearst makes a difference, doesn't he? Admit it."

Savage felt as though he had been suddenly doused with cold water.

"Of course I admit it," he answered abruptly. "Excuse me. I want to check on Tony's Charley horse. He got hit there again."

He walked away, leaving Cal Murchison looking after him with a strangely speculative expression.

11

THAT the Cavaliers were smack in the middle of the Rose Bowl picture was increasingly clear to Savage as the week began. " Beat the Hurricanes " stickers blossomed on windshields and walls all over the campus, and newspapers outside the immediate vicinity began to take a sharpened interest in the Cavaliers.

He was also deluged with telephone calls and letters from persons who wanted to enlist his help in getting tickets to the game. Some could claim friendship, some were acquaintances whom he hadn't seen since his undergraduate days, some were complete strangers.

" A man doesn't know how many buddies he has until times like these," he exclaimed wearily to LaCosta, holding up one letter. " Here's a joker who says we were on the same troop transport going to Japan five years ago, and naturally I remember him. All he wants is four tickets, and they must be high up and not outside the 30-yard line. I swear I don't know him from a sack of cement."

" He won't know you either, if we lose," was Sam's dour reply. But even he seemed affected by the rising tide of excitement that engulfed students and players alike as game time drew nearer.

It was difficult, in such an atmosphere, to view the Hurricane strength dispassionately. But Babe Bassich, who had scouted the Rossiter game, made it clear that Mount Royal was rugged.

"They got the break Saturday, yes," he conceded. "But Hacker is the best split-T quarter I've seen all year — even better than he was last year, and he killed us then."

"How did Rossiter play him?"

"They put one man on him — Klipstein, the center — to crack him on every play, whether he had the ball or not. He followed Hacker as though Andy owed him money. And Klipstein weighs 215. He wore him down some, but Hacker is tough. Any split-T quarterback has to be, these days."

"It didn't work, then?" Savage asked, frowning.

"Oh, sure it worked, but not well enough," Babe said. "I think Crump would have got the job done better, because he's quicker than Klipstein. Last year — you remember, George — we were more afraid of the halfbacks and we set the defense for the wide stuff."

Breck nodded. "Hacker ran us silly on the keeps. You can't play him straightaway. I'd say our best chance is to do what Rossiter did, except we'd do it with Vince. What do you think, Sam?"

LaCosta gave Savage a quick glance.

"Seems the best way, I suppose," he said slowly.

Savage knew what Sam was thinking. Give Crump a single target and you were inviting trouble. And yet it was an obvious move, strength against strength. He shook off his misgivings. There had been no untoward incidents in the last two games. Surely Vince knew by now that he was a marked man. Mean and tough, yes, but with too much hard common sense to do anything foolish.

"Yes, let's do it that way," he said, and Breck smiled in

approval. Sam's face was expressionless.

They tried the defense in scrimmage with Frederickson portraying Hacker, and the first string made it look good. Frederickson was unashamedly happy when it ended.

"Man, am I glad I won't be Hacker on Saturday," he announced as they trudged to the showers. "I wouldn't want that Vince living with me on every play."

"Aw, he was only walking through it today," Mahoney scoffed. "When he lays the wood and means it, you'll know it, Freddie."

Crump, who had overheard, gave Mahoney a grin.

There was more to the preparation than devising ways of halting Hacker, of course. Savage added a few knick-knacks he had been saving as a gift package for Rossiter, but there was no percentage in withholding anything now.

So the Cavaliers drilled on a series from the tight-T formation, a tackle-eligible pass play, and a pass off a double reverse — none of which they had shown before. One of them or all of them might catch Mount Royal off balance and be worth six points.

The Cavaliers rose to the game by themselves. The problem was to keep them from being keyed too high. Savage did his best.

"Forget all this yammer about the Rose Bowl," he advised them in the last expectant moment before they went out on the field. "You're not in Pasadena; you're in your own stadium and playing a team called Mount Royal. They can be had. So let's go out and have 'em."

The coaches followed the squad onto the turf, hearing the roar that greeted its appearance.

"The hay's in the barn now," Savage said. "Too late to teach 'em anything more."

"It's the same over there," LaCosta said, gesturing toward the Mount Royal bench. " Bill Evers is asking himself, ' What did I forget to tell them? ' "

Breck said: " The boys want this one bad. I've got a hunch they're gonna get it, Ed."

Savage encountered Evers, the Hurricane coach, as they wandered in mid-field during the warmup. Evers, a grizzled campaigner, lighted and extinguished two cigarettes during the brief time in which they exchanged commonplace remarks.

Sam's right, Savage thought. The man is just as jumpy as I am, and he's been through this wringer a hundred times.

He wondered if a coach ever learned how to take pressure games in stride. He hoped so.

Eventually, the officials beckoned to the game captains — Glass today for the Cavaliers, a sturdy guard named Jones for Mount Royal — for the toss of the coin. Mount Royal won, chose to receive, and as the Hastings rooting section came to its feet screaming, Whitney sent the ball sailing in a long arc down toward the goal posts.

The constricted feeling in Savage's throat eased as Maderas crashed the receiver with a jarring tackle on the 22. As he squatted on his haunches in front of the bench, he was suddenly calmer than he had been all week. This was still a game for schoolboys, despite the sixty thousand people in the stands. The world would not end if Hastings lost.

He was glad the Hurricanes had elected to receive, for they, too, were taut with eagerness. The left end jumped off side on the first play and cost them five; a halfback mishandled the ball on the dive-tackle play and was fortunate to hang on to it. When Brodsky, the fullback, dropped back to punt and Glass let the ball roll dead on the Hastings 36, Savage felt that the first dangerous hurdle had been cleared. The Cavaliers had been given time to settle down.

It developed into a bruising duel between two stubborn defenses. What Mount Royal's line lacked in size it made up in agility, and its secondary was swift and alert. Hastings did not cross mid-field in the first half; only once could the Hurricanes make two first downs in a row.

Crump shadowed Hacker like a Federal agent, crashing him on the spins, the keeps, and the infrequent roll-out passes. It was rough, but it was legitimate, and it seemed to have no visible effect on Hacker physically. He came up after every tackle as thought he welcomed more.

Vince did not hold off the Hurricanes alone, to be sure. Casper, playing his best game of the season, submarined the plays up the middle in magnificent fashion; Hearst slammed into the off-tackle slants like a falling wall and first Maderas, then Bedolla, turned the pitchouts to the inside with smart, sure-handed maneuvering.

They look like a team that's been coached, Savage thought with a sense of pride. The three of them — Sam, George, and himself — had done that much of a job, if nothing else.

He couldn't say as much for the offense, which was primarily the responsibility of the head coach. The switch to the tight-T, with its different line-spacing, had not disturbed the Hurricanes a whit. As for the other tricks, Hastings had not been close enough to scoring territory to warrant their use.

Mount Royal struck suddenly, soon after the second half opened. Clawson developed a painful but not disabling leg cramp that forced him to the side lines. While Dave Rolph was expertly kneading the knotted muscles, the Hurricanes came up with a halfback pass off a pitchout.

It caught Murdock, the second-string center, out of

141

position, and the receiver weaved his way down to the Cavalier 22-yard line before Glass and Corbett dropped him.

Savage plucked nervously at the grass in front of him, silently echoing the exhortation from the stands to "Get that ball!"

The Cavaliers didn't quite accomplish that, but they did force Mount Royal to settle for less than it wanted. The Hurricanes drove to the 11 as Hacker worked a delayed quarterback draw for six, one of the few times he successfully evaded Crump.

But three plays later they were only on the 6, as the red-jerseys dug in grimly. On fourth down, the ball lay directly in front of the goal posts and Mount Royal took what it could get. Hacker knelt on the 14 and Brodsky kicked it out of his hold for the three points.

Savage, disappointed but not discouraged, felt a hand on his elbow. It was Clawson, straining at the leash.

"I want in there, Coach," he said.

"Easy does it, Bob. How's the leg?"

"Nothing but a cramp. Good as new. Three points won't win this, I'll guarantee that."

Savage sent him on his way after giving him a brief rundown to be relayed to Glass. LaCosta, on the stadium rim, thought he had detected a pattern in the stunting tactics of the Hurricane defense. If he was correct, the Cavaliers had plays that should work.

They got a rolling start as Travis, after taking the kickoff on the 5, appeared to be hemmed in near the 20, only to spin loose and fight his way up to the 36.

Glass, taking the bit in his teeth, gambled on the pass down the slot to the flanker back and Corbett, although hit solidly as he caught, hung on for the first down at the 50.

142

That was the Cavaliers' deepest penetration of the day, and it raised the rooting section to a frenzied chant of " Go, go, go! " No one was seated on the Hastings bench; the substitutes lined the side line, screaming encouragement.

Glass moved them. Hastings had been starting on a medium long count, four to eight numbers before the ball was snapped, and the left defensive side of the Hurricanes had been jumping around, in and out of the line, during that interval.

This time the Cavaliers went right after Glass had called " Set! " Hearst caught the tackle moving to the inside as Maderas came across to crack the line backer. Whitney got a shoulder into the end and moved him to the outside. The lane was open and Travis came barreling through it, slanting to his right as Corbett, racing with him on the inside, screened off the halfback.

Junior was no fancy stepper in the open, but in full stride he was hard to bring down. The Hurricane safety dove for his legs, and he made a full pivot to twist loose. But the pursuit had time to gain on him, and he finally went down on the Mount Royal 19.

Glass had to gesture to his own rooters to quiet down so that his signals could be heard. Savage, his pulses throbbing, shouted for Fitzgerald. This was the spot for the tackle-eligible pass, if ever there was one. In an exciting moment, more than one veteran quarterback had been known to forget all about certain plays.

But even as he dug his fingers into Fitz's arm, ready to shove him in on the next down, Savage saw that Glass had not forgotten.

The Cavaliers came out in their regular flanker-T formation. As Glass counted, " Set, one, two! " Whitney, on the short side, dropped back a step and Corbett moved up to

143

the line outside Maderas' shoulder.

That made Mahoney an end for the moment. The Cavaliers went on the very next count, giving the Hurricanes as little time as possible to adjust to the shift.

Glass faked to Freeman, retreated three steps, and threw to the spot where Mahoney was supposed to be, six yards past the line of scrimmage. The big tackle was there and the pass hit him chest-high.

He turned and began to run, if his movements could be described as running. To Savage, it seemed as though Mike was moving in slow motion, but in his lumbering, heavy-footed fashion he did move, all the way down to the 5-yard line.

It took three plays to get over from there. The Hurricanes bowed their backs and dug their cleats into the turf, but Hastings was fired too high to be halted. Freeman slammed at right guard for one; Glass, burrowing like a mole behind the charge of Crump and Clawson, sneaked for one plus. Then as Glass leaped high on the fake of a jump pass, Travis blasted at tackle and went stumbling and falling on hands and knees into the end zone. The stadium became a huge cavern of unintelligible sound.

Savage, face flushed with exuberance, eyes shining, dared not breathe as Whitney swung his leg experimentally and sighted for the try for point. It sailed straight and true for 7–3, and Savage suddenly felt limp all over. To him, it was the most satisfying touchdown of the season. Hastings had demonstrated that it could come from behind.

But it was far from finished. Enough time remained to win or lose three games. And Mount Royal wanted this one.

Just how badly they wanted it became evident quickly. Hearst failed to get up after the second play, and came off

144

with uncertain steps between Doc Beardsley and Dave Rolph.

"Wind knocked out of him, that's all," the doctor said in answer to Savage's anxious query. "He'll be all right in a few minutes."

Hearst was muttering angrily as he eased his long frame to the ground.

"That's twice he gave me the fist," he complained through puffed lips. "Next time —"

"Never mind next time," Savage said. "If there's any funny business, it's your last time, remember that. Now relax, kid."

He turned back to watch the action with increasing disquiet. There was trouble in the air.

It flared openly a moment later as Hacker, dipping in and out on the roll-out, couldn't find an open receiver and began to run. Crump, trailing him, grabbed him high, pinioning his arms in a bear hug.

The referee whistled the play dead, but Vince, maintaining his hold, pushed Hacker backward for another five yard. When he released his grip, Hacker, visibly nettled, gave him a half shove. Crump started back toward him, but the referee came between them at once, said something in a firm manner, and they separated. The Hastings stands began to jeer at Hacker.

"Give it to him, Vince!" a player behind Savage urged in excitement. Breck said softly, "Looks like things are beginning to heat up, Ed."

Savage wavered. He ought to pull Crump out right now for that prep-school trick. Vince knew that even had he pushed Hacker all the way back to the end zone, the ball would be brought back to the point where the runner had originally been stopped.

As Savage hesitated, the Hurricane fullback slashed into

the secondary on a quick-opener. Savage reached for the press-box phone.

"Inside Fairchild," Sam said laconically. "He played the end head on and the guy took him alone. Casper's used up too. They'll hammer that spot."

"O.K., I'll get Sonny out."

Fitzgerald went in at middle guard, and a weary Casper came off the field, rubbing a bruised knuckle.

"That No. 53 keeps reaching under my face guard," he said angrily. "He likes it so much, I let him try a sample."

Savage shut his ears to it. Why didn't Bill Evers keep his Hurricanes under control? This could be the Linfield game all over again if it got any worse.

The Mount Royal right halfback swung outside for good yardage, but Maderas was rolling on the ground clutching his leg in pain, and the referee was pacing off fifteen yards for clipping against the Hurricanes. Evers stalked the opposite side line like a caged animal.

Sid limped off and Savage knew, with a sinking feeling, that the end was through for the day.

The penalty was enough to force Mount Royal to punt. Travis, slanting for four yards, went down under a mass of tacklers, and when a Hurricane halfback flung himself on top of the pile after the whistle, the visitors drew another fifteen-yarder for unnecessary roughness.

"They'll knock themselves right out of this game," Savage said grimly to Breck. "If we just keep our heads and don't try to foul with them."

Even with the penalty, Hastings could not cross the midfield mark. Glass, trying for the coffin corner, just missed it. The ball rolled into the end zone and Mount Royal started from the 20 as the quarter ended.

Hearst was on his feet again, jogging up and down and

eager to return. Given the nod of assent from Doc Beards-ley, Savage sent Larry in.

Mount Royal plunged for one first down, but found the soft spot at tackle no longer soft, and Hacker began to pass with greater frequency. He forsook the roll-out and dropped straight back from center, throwing from behind a protective cup of blockers. And he began to complete them.

They were short ones, true — swing passes, side-line throws and buttonhooks, difficult to defend against, although the Cavalier secondary hit the receivers almost as soon as they caught and limited the gain.

But Hacker completed them, nevertheless, amazingly cool under the fierce charge of the Hastings forwards. He got the ball away, but by such narrow margins that he was invariably knocked down at once by Crump or Hearst or Bedolla.

Not once could they reach him in time, however, and from its 20, Mount Royal moved inexorably downfield — to the 40, the 50, the Cavalier 36.

Watching, Savage had the strange, detached feeling that the Hurricanes were going all the way. There were times when a good team simply would not be denied, when everything a great player like Hacker did seemed touched with magic. This was one of them.

Using the running play just often enough to keep the defense honest, Hacker sent his fullback bucking at guard for four yards. The swing pass to the flanker was held to one as Corbett trailed the receiver all the way.

Hacker took the snapback and backed up quickly as red jerseys poured in on his blockers. The Hurricane right end, checked momentarily at the line, broke straight down and then out toward the side line.

Hacker's arm went up and back and the ball went sailing out toward the end, two steps in front of Corbett. Savage's eyes followed its flight, saw the end leap high to pull it down and be tumbled to earth at once. But instinctively, from his line of sight, he knew that the catch had been made out of bounds. Hacker had thrown the ball just a little too far.

His judgment was confirmed at once, as the field judge on the far side line and nearest the receiver signaled that the pass was incomplete.

"Fourth and five, George," Savage said tensely. "This is the big one."

But Breck's gaze was fixed on the field, and Savage looked. Two white-shirted Hurricane players were bending over an inert figure back of the line of scrimmage, and a third was beckoning frantically toward the Mount Royal bench.

"Who is it?" Savage's voice was husky.

"Hacker, I think." Breck did not turn his head.

Let's hope he gets up quickly — Savage made it almost a prayer. He went to the phone as the Hurricanes' doctor and trainer hurried onto the field, followed by Evers.

"What happened, Sam? Did you see it?"

LaCosta said, in a voice charged with emotion: "It's Hacker. Crump went over him after he got the ball away. I couldn't tell how it happened, Ed."

"I see."

Hacker was still down and the doctor was examining him. It could be anything, Savage told himself. The defense had the right to crash the passer while he was still in the act of throwing. Hacker was shaken up, or a leg had twisted under him, or maybe he was just worn out. Something ordinary, that could occur on any play in good, hard football.

back to the camera, was Crump, shoulders hunched. He was a step closer to Hacker than Bedolla. That was all; the next frames picked up the receiver and the Hastings defender.

"That's the play on which Hacker was hurt, isn't it?" Babe Bassich asked. He had been scouting Rossiter, but he knew.

"Yes, that's the play," Savage said. He did not elaborate. The next person to know that Vince Crump had played his last game for Hastings had to be Vince himself. And telling him was not going to be easy.

~

Crump sat in the chair, facing Savage across the desk. He seemed completely relaxed, but his heavy-lidded eyes were alert, inquiring. To be called to the coach's office in the deserted gym on a Sunday afternoon was unusual. Something was in the air, and he was wary.

"Vince, you broke Andy Hacker's jaw."

Savage delivered it as a statement, unemotionally, with no accusatory inflection. It jerked Crump erect in the chair as though he had been jabbed with a needle. He leaned forward, jaw outthrust, eyes alive with anger, even his close-cropped cap of hair seeming to bristle.

"That's not the way it was, Mister!" he ripped out. "His jaw got busted. Maybe it was me who hit him, maybe somebody else. Whatever, it was an accident. Tough on Andy, sure, but accidental. You got any proof it wasn't?"

"They've been too many accidents in your vicinity," Savage said. A vein in his temple pulsed rhythmically; his own temper was near the bursting point. "I'm not going to risk another. You won't play against Rossiter."

Crump's hands grasped the arms of his chair and Savage

153

tensed, half expecting the guard to spring at him. Vince's face was a dull red; the white scar on his cheek stood out as though it had been painted there.

"You can't pull that on me!" he said through clenched teeth. "I've earned the right to play in that game, and the Rose Bowl too. You can't take it away from me just like that. If it weren't for me, you wouldn't even be close to the Rose Bowl, and you know it!"

Savage leaned across the desk, his gray eyes flinty.

"Let's lay it out where we can both look at it, Vince. I've made mistakes, and the biggest one was not putting a halter on you early, the day you racked up Joe Scarsella. Sure, you're a whale of a football player, but football isn't war. There are some things that don't go, Vince, accidents or not. You try that stuff in pro ball, and you'll be an accident all by yourself. They know how to handle that stuff."

Crump sneered. "A real character builder, eh?"

Savage let it pass.

"Now about Rossiter. Get this straight. I run the team — maybe good, maybe not — but I run it. You don't play."

"And how are you going to explain that?" Vince demanded harshly.

"That's up to you. I can drop you publicly for dirty play, but I'd rather not. Let's say you got hurt Saturday — a knee, maybe. In that case, only Doc Beardsley and a few others need know the truth. Now, how do you want it — hard or easy?"

Crump glared at him in unconcealed hatred, his jaw muscles working convulsively. He could see that Savage meant business. For seconds, the silence seemed charged with electricity. Then he spoke, in a voice choked with emotion.

"All right, I'll buy it. It's a raw, dirty deal, but you've got a gun at my head. I have to buy it, you —"

Something in Savage's expression warned him not to say it. He rose abruptly, almost knocking over the chair.

"I hope Rossiter beats your brains out," he flung at Savage. "And they will!"

Then he was gone, slamming the door hard. Savage felt a momentary shakiness, like the remembered reaction after a successful mission over enemy lines. His hands were trembling a little, and he sat quietly for a moment, steadying his nerves. He was almost certain Crump would not talk; Vince was proud of his toughness, but not so proud that he would be willing to risk a public accusation of this sort.

There remained the delicate task of informing the persons who had to know the facts — Dr. Beardsley, in the event he was questioned on the nature of Vince's supposed injury, the coaches, and of course, Cal Murchison. To everyone else — the newspapers and the players — it would be simply a bad knee.

Dr. Beardsley agreed with reluctance.

"I am not questioning your action," he said heavily, "but I dislike the subterfuge it involves on my part. Under the circumstances, however, I will go along."

"Thank you, Doctor. I would not have asked you to do this if I did not believe that in this case subterfuge was the least harmful to everyone concerned."

The coaches gathered again Sunday evening to go over Bassich's report on Rossiter, and Savage broke the news to them when they had finished.

Sam LaCosta, to whom it did not come as a surprise, took it with no change of expression. Bassich's eyes reflected amazement, but he merely grunted.

To George Breck, however, it was as though he had been struck. A flush spread slowly over his thin, hawklike face.

"You can't mean it, Ed?" he said incredulously. "Dropping Vince? Now, with Rossiter coming up? You can't!"

"I can, and I have, George." Savage's voice was flat, hard. "I've already called Jake Gledhill and Roy Caster to tell them he's hurt and won't play Saturday. And he won't."

"I see." Breck looked almost appealingly at Bassich, then at LaCosta, and realized that he stood alone.

"You're the boss, Ed," he said. "It will be an awful jolt to the team, though. They depend on Vince in the tight spots. He's their leader."

"It will have to be a jolt, then."

"Suppose it gets out that he really could play?" Breck pursued anxiously. "Have you thought about that?"

"Yes, I have. Seven persons know the truth, and one of them is Vince. But I don't care if he broadcasts it from a sound trucks in the streets — he does not play."

He spoke the last words slowly and emphatically and Breck realized the futility of argument.

George really doesn't understand, Savage thought. It was not his fault; he was simply a product of the system that made winning more rewarding than losing. The coaching ranks were full of George Brecks — honest, decent men by the standards of the profession, and many of them became head coaches. Savage supposed George would be, in time. He was a competent man.

He kept Cal Murchison to the last, telephoning him at home. When Cal answered, Savage could hear the sound of voices in the background. The athletic director said in disbelief, "You what?" when Savage had explained the reason he had called.

"I don't see that I had any other choice, Cal."

Murchison dropped his voice. "I have some guests, Ed, I can't discuss it now. But I want to see you — tomorrow morning, early. Let's say nine at my office."

"At nine, Cal. I'll be there."

~~

The chimes in the Hastings chapel tower were striking the last note of nine when Savage entered Murchison's office. The athletic director, gazing out the window toward the gym, turned and said lightly: " Beautiful morning, Ed. Have a chair."

But there were grave lines in his face as he seated himself at his desk.

" Ed, I wish you had consulted me before giving out this story about Vince. It's a very touchy situation."

Cal had a point, Savage conceded.

"There had to be a reason why Crump isn't playing," he explained. " I wanted to furnish one before the reporters started asking questions. I think they'll accept it."

Murchison frowned, drumming fingers on his desk.

" Ed, don't you think the injury to Hacker could have been accidental? "

Savage stared.

" You saw the game, Cal. What did you think? "

" I don't know, frankly. I can't believe Vince would do such a thing deliberately, and I'd hesitate to make the charge without absolute proof. Do you have that? "

Savage shifted uneasily in his chair.

" Short of an affidavit from Crump himself, I don't know how you'd get the kind of proof you might need in a court of law," he answered. " I'm convinced in my own mind, though. Do you think I'd drop my best player before the Rossiter game if there were any other course open to me? "

" I know how you feel, Ed. What chance do we have Saturday without Crump? "

" I suppose they'll run up the middle on us pretty well."

"And if he did play, what would our chances be?"

Savage's eyes narrowed.

"Better, but still not good," he replied coldly. "But why speculate? He isn't."

"Now, Ed, let's not be bullheaded," Murchison said in a soothing manner. "There are other factors to be considered. This is a big thing for Hastings. A chance for the Rose Bowl. Do you appreciate how much that means to our students, our alumni? I haven't seen such enthusiasm, such pride in a team in twenty years. I realize we may lose to Rossiter anyway, but why throw away your best card before the draw on mere suspicion? There's too much at stake, Ed."

I shouldn't really be surprised, Savage thought dully. I should have seen this coming. Yet disillusion stung him like a whip.

"You want me to play him, then?"

"Why not?" Murchison spread his hands in an expansive gesture. "Larry Hearst slugged a man; you put him back. Even if Vince was guilty, he deserves a second chance — you've said that yourself."

Savage looked at Cal, at his strong, tanned, still youthful face, as though he were seeing it for the first time.

"Cal, I can't do it." He had to force the words out of his throat and saw the look of pained astonishment they evoked.

"Ed, I'm asking this as a friend," he said heavily. "Not for myself, but for the school. A favor. Don't you think you owe me one?"

Savage's face was haggard. Murchison alone was responsible for his present position of importance. But suddenly Cal was changing the ground rules on him. This was not why he had come to Hastings. If he had had the courage to stand fast from the beginning, to steer the course he had

158

first set, he would not be sitting here now with this feeling of hollowness.

Yes, he owed Cal a great deal. But he did not owe him that much.

"No, Cal." He almost whispered it. "No. Crump is out."

He rose swiftly and went out, not waiting for, nor wanting to hear, Murchison's next words.

As he crossed the courtyard between the athletic director's office and his own in the gym, he heard his name shouted, and spun around to confront the rumpled figure of Jake Gledhill.

"Hello, Jake." He made an effort to sound cordial. "Aren't you up and around pretty early?"

"Something I want to show you," Gledhill said enigmatically, tapping a large manila envelope under his arm. "Can we retire to your cozy quarters?"

Once inside the office, Savage said, "All right, what is it?"

"Bad break about Crump," Jake said casually, ignoring the question. "He'll be missed. I suppose Fitzgerald will start?"

"Probably. He's been coming along. He'll be all right."

Gledhill took out his pipe, began to tap it absently against his palm.

"You know, I saw Vince in the dressing room Saturday and he didn't look like a man with a bad knee. He seemed to be walking naturally. Anything happen to him after that?"

He regarded Savage blandly.

"Not that I know of." Savage stiffened, hating the need to maintain the untruth. "Delayed reaction. It stiffened up on him yesterday. I've seen that happen many times."

"Oh, sure. Hurts your chances a lot, I'd say."

His nerves raw, Savage rasped: "Crump's good, but

159

he's not that good! We're not conceding a thing. Anything can happen in a Rossiter game and you ought to know it, Jake. You've seen enough of them."

"I certainly have, and that's a popular misconception." Jake seemed unruffled. "The underdog comes through with the upset in the traditional game — records don't count. But if you check back, you'll find it isn't true. Nine times out of ten, the favorite — the team with the horses — wins the Hastings–Rossiter game."

He tossed the envelope on Savage's desk.

"Thought you might like to see this. We had three photogs working Saturday. Link Adams took this one from the side lines. I almost ran it Sunday morning, but decided not to. Old school tie, you know. Keep it for your memory book."

He was gone before Savage could think of anything to say. Mechanically, he opened the envelope and extracted an enlarged print of a picture, eight inches by eleven. One glance, and he sucked in his breath sharply.

There, in dreadful clarity, was the evidence. Hacker's arm was on the way down; the picture had been taken a split second after the movie camera had shifted to follow the ball, and from a different angle.

To the upper left was the figure of Chuck Bedolla, arms raised in his vain attempt to block the pass. Crump was in the center, only a step away from the quarterback. His face was turned away from the camera, but clearly visible against the darker background was the clenched right fist, poised like a boxer's.

Once he understood what he held in his hand, Savage's first impulse was to take it to Murchison and fling it down before him.

No, that wouldn't help, he reflected sadly. Cal was concerned only with Crump's usefulness, not with his guilt

160

or innocence. It must have cost him something in self-respect to ask the favor, Savage realized. To confront him with the picture now could only humiliate him further. And Savage did not want to do that.

He could hardly condemn Murchison. He had deluded himself about Vince Crump, knowing but not wanting to know, trying to justify Vince's actions in his mind because Vince was important to Hastings' success.

Well, he knew now, and so did Jake Gledhill.

Slowly and methodically, he tore the picture in strips, those strips into smaller ones, and dropped them into a wastebasket.

13

TO Savage's surprised relief, the team as a whole took the news of Crump's loss with more poise than he could have hoped for. The general reaction was one of sympathy for Crump, although all of them realized his absence Saturday would not improve their chances. It was a jolt, yes, but its impact was lighter than anticipated.

It's still the Rossiter game, Savage thought. And it's still Homecoming Week. I've forgotten that these are still kids. They bounce.

During the long chalk-talk, though, he caught Bob Clawson looking at him oddly, and Sonny Whitney seemed to be listening in a preoccupied manner.

Then, after practice, Sid Maderas asked if anyone had seen old Vince.

" I went round to his room at the dorm after lunch to see how he was," the halfback said, " but there was nobody in. Is he in the infirmary? "

" No," Clawson answered abruptly. " I checked."

Maderas remarked that seemed strange and Savage moved on with a feeling of uneasiness. Either Clawson knew the truth or he suspected something.

But whatever Crump meant to the team, his presence

or absence made only a glancing impression on the thousands of Hastings students. This was the week of the traditional big game, and the campus came alive to those traditions as it had each year, regardless of the outlook for victory or defeat. To the undergraduates, the outlook for Saturday was still brighter than it had been within their memory, and the loss of one player could not dim it very much.

There were rallies and dances and alumni reunions on the campus, all the trappings of Homecoming Week. It mounted to its climax on Thursday night outside the stadium, when the wood gathered so painstakingly by the freshmen was ignited in a huge bonfire.

Savage stood on a temporary platform with the flickering light illuminating his features and made the traditional speech to the massed young and eager faces below him.

It was a short speech, but he spoke of spirit and honor and the Hastings heritage — all the intangibles which could mean so much to some, nothing at all to others.

" Win or lose, I know you will be proud of this team on Saturday," he concluded, and they cheered him mightily. He had told them what they wanted to hear, given lip service to the shadowy ideals of sportsmanship and fair play. All over the country, he thought bleakly, coaches were making the same kind of speech on the eve of the big game. It was part of the job, whether they believed a word of it or not.

Savage himself did not have the slightest idea whether the Cavaliers would make it close. During the week's practice, he had seen the nervous excitement stirring in some of the players, like Fitzgerald and Kassowitz and Hearst, who had never before played in a Rossiter game.

But there were no signs of it among the veterans — Clawson, Mahoney, Whitney, and the others. To be sure, they had been there before. But Savage felt that something else lay beneath their apparent lack of enthusiasm — the uncertainty of playing without Vince Crump, who seemed to have simply vanished. From the snatches of conversation he had overheard, Savage knew that none of the players had seen him, and that they were baffled and disturbed by that.

Savage came off the platform, smiling mechanically as he moved through the crowd, now beginning to disperse. Occasionally he stopped to shake hands or acknowledge a cheerful greeting. He was near the fringe of the dissolving mass when he saw Murchison, standing motionless as though waiting for him.

" Good rally, don't you think? " Cal asked quietly.

" Real good one, Cal."

" Haven't changed your mind, I suppose."

Savage sighed.

" I can't, Cal," he said pleadingly. " Don't you see that I can't? "

In the darkness, he could not make out Murchison's features, but he saw Cal's shoulders sag a little, as though he was very tired.

" Yes, I see, Ed," he answered in a low voice. " I envy you. I really do."

He turned and walked away slowly, and Savage was suddenly very sorry for Cal Murchison, who envied him the freedom to act according to what he believed, without compromise. Like George Breck, Murchison was an honest man, the victim of forces that had grown too powerful for the simple schoolboy sport of football.

Savage imagined that Cal had brought to his job a youthful fervor of ideas and ideals of his own. Little by little, they had been chipped away by the necessities of an ath-

164

letic plant requiring support in hundreds of thousands of dollars.

At some point in his career, Cal must have been faced with the choice between principle and the practical — what was right and what would work. He had, under what pressures Savage could only conjecture, chosen the practical. From that time on, it had governed his thinking, and now he was too old to change. He knew it. That was why he envied Savage.

Standing alone in the darkness, Savage realized that it would soon be too late for him too. He had followed the path of least resistance long enough to see where it led. Coaches as highly paid as he could not afford the luxury of losing. That could be indulged only at a small school, like Niles. And the work there had been fun, but offering no challenge, nothing to which a man could devote his entire life.

Sarah Fleming had been right — a man ought to test his own capabilities to the limit, not settle for less out of laziness or lack of courage. He had wanted to be a doctor, but he had shied away from the hard work and the sacrifice that demanded.

So he had come to Hastings, believing there was a good and worth-while job to be done, and he had failed at that. He had taught his players how to block, how to tackle — no more than that. He had earned neither their friendship nor their trust, and he had done nothing to deserve them.

I'd better get out, he thought with sudden resolve. Now, while there's still time.

It would be difficult to pick up the threads of academic life again, to face the years of intensive studying in comparative poverty, but he was going to be a doctor. At least he was going to try.

The thought that Sarah Fleming would approve gave him a strangely warming feeling. What Sarah believed was suddenly very important.

—

The muffled ringing of the telephone in the adjoining room woke Savage on Saturday morning. He looked at his watch and was mildly surprised to see that it was nearly nine o'clock. He had slept like a child.

LaCosta's stocky figure appeared in the doorway.

"You must have a clear conscience, sleeping like that," he commented sarcastically. "Do you want to talk to a lady or do I tell her you're still sacked out?"

"Sarah? I'll talk."

He got out of bed and padded into the living room. La-Costa, already dressed, muttered that he'd heat up the coffee and went into the kitchen.

"As usual, I wanted to wish you luck," Sarah said. "Were you really asleep this late? Today, the most important game of the season? I'm amazed."

"Thank you, doll. I really was asleep, and I will tell you why. The game is not that important."

"Not important?" She sounded bewildered. "Are you joking?"

"I am not. It is not important because it will very probably be my last one. I'm quitting, Sarah."

He heard her give a little gasp.

"You do mean it, I can tell." Her voice was a little shaky. "But why — what made you decide now? And what are you going to do, Ed?"

"It's a long story. I'm going back to medical school. That's what I should have done three years ago."

"Oh, Ed," she breathed. Then: "Please come and tell me everything. I want to help. Will you let me help, Ed?"

"We can talk about it, Sarah," he said softly. "We can talk about a lot of things, I think."

"When? Tonight?"

"Why not tonight? About seven? I'll pick you up."

"Seven o'clock. That seems a long time to wait."

"Well, it has to be seven o'clock eventually. Just one thing, doll. You're the first to know. Keep it to yourself. O.K.?"

"O.K, And, Ed — good luck today, anyway."

Savage looked thoughtful as he hung up. If Hastings won today, then in all fairness he must wait until after the Rose Bowl game to make public his decision. The kids would have earned it if they did win; it would not be right to clutter their minds with the uncertainties of their coach's future.

If Hastings lost today, then he would tell Murchison at once and leave it up to Cal how to handle the announcement. But one other person deserved to know now — Sam LaCosta. Sam was his responsibility.

He went into the bedroom and returned holding a sealed envelope just as Sam emerged from the kitchen with the coffee urn. Savage laid the letter on the table.

"This is my resignation, Sam. It will be on Cal's desk Monday morning if Rossiter beats us."

LaCosta set the coffee urn down carefully and regarded Savage steadily.

"And if we win?"

"Then he gets it the day after New Year's, win, lose, or draw. On that, my mind's made up, Sam."

"Too rich for your blood too, is that it?"

"In a way, Sam, but for a reason different from yours," Savage said. "I'm going to be the world's oldest living med student."

LaCosta's heavy brows went up.

167

"Ah. So that's the way it is."

"That's the way it is. I'll spell it out for you whenever you like, but not this morning. I thought if you knew, though, it might help you settle things in your own mind. You could stay here, you know — you might even be the head man. Would that tempt you?"

LaCosta shook his head.

"It sounds better than it is, Ed, you know that. I told you I was just a country boy. Sure, I want to be a head coach, but not in this league unless it's on my own terms. I doubt that Hastings would meet them. Nope, it's me for the tall corn. I reached that decision a couple of days ago; this move of yours doesn't have anything to do with it. So don't bother your pointed head about me. I mean it."

Relief showed in Savage's face.

"I'm glad of that, Sam."

"I don't think I'll regret it. I've a hunch you won't regret yours, either."

Savage picked up the letter and hefted it in one hand as though it were a heavy object.

"Remind me to buy stamps, will you, Sam?" he said smilingly.

—

Glass came into the dressing room humming the Hastings marching song and did a little jig step as he went to his locker.

"Ready, Al?" Savage inquired, amused. The quarterback made an "O" of thumb and forefinger.

"Ready and able, Coach."

They followed Glass in groups of two and three. Some of them, like Hearst and Kassowitz, had the bright, feverish look of anticipation; others, like Fitzgerald, were obviously jumpy. Fitz went to the drinking fountain three times before starting to unbutton his shirt.

Savage stepped out of the room and went to the trainer's quarters. Through the window he watched the people beginning to stream past on the way to the stadium entrances.

Leave 'em alone, he thought. Sam and George and Dave Rolph would supervise the taping; he had nothing more to tell them. The field strategy had been worked out during the week; the quarterbacks knew what to try, and when — if Rossiter would permit. The Raiders had two units, one as good as the other at most positions, and man for man superior to the Cavaliers' one-deep team in all but two or three spots.

An indestructible animal like Crump could help balance the scales, as he had all season. But instead of Vince, it had to be Fitzgerald. Only a few of the thousands in the stands would see the difference; nearly everyone watched the ball carrier. They did not notice what was happening to the linemen.

But Rossiter would know the difference — knew it already. And so did the Cavalier squad. Still, Savage was glad he was going with Fitzgerald. Whether or not Fitz got the job done, he would not disappoint.

Savage was still gazing out the window when Breck came for him.

" It's one fifteen, Ed. We ought to be getting out there."

Breck had a resigned air, like a man prepared for the worst. If some of the players — Vince's admirers, for instance — felt that way, it could be bad. In any case, he wasn't going to make an oration. If a Hastings team did not come up by itself for a Rossiter game, words would be wasted.

So he faced them and said quite casually: " This is the first big game for some of you and the last one for some others. Let's make it one you'd like to remember. Lead 'em out, Al."

There was a moment of stunned silence; obviously they had expected more. Glass, the game captain, looked at Savage wonderingly, as though he was not sure the coach was finished. Then he said, "Let's go, fellows," and in silent puzzlement the red-jerseyed file began to shuffle out.

"That was a short one, Ed," Breck said.

"I mislaid the notes for my long one," Savage answered, and followed Dave Rolph through the doorway.

The warmup period ended and the Hastings and Rossiter bands massed in mid-field to play "The Star-spangled Banner." As the officials beckoned the captains for the toss of the coin, Savage felt a light touch on his arm. He turned to face a serious-looking Bob Clawson.

"I'd like to say something about Vince," he began in a hesitant manner, and Savage stiffened instinctively. "He's really not a bad guy, but some of us thought it was too bad about Andy Hacker. We were sorry it happened and we wrote Andy a letter about it. He's missing a big game too."

Clawson stumbled over the words, as though he found them difficult. As their meaning penetrated, the tight lines around Savage's mouth smoothed away and he knew a deep glow of gratitude. So Crump's friends knew the real reason why Vince was not there, and agreed it was fitting he should not be.

"Thanks for telling me, Bob."

Clawson looked uncomfortable. "I thought you ought to know. Anyway, we're not going to give this game away, I promise you that. I'd like to see the Rose Bowl from the inside. And for free."

They didn't give it away, even after Travis, tackled with terrific impact on the kickoff return, dropped the ball and Rossiter recovered on the 16-yard line.

Klein, the Raider fullback, took his shot at left guard. Fitzgerald, dropping into the line at the last second, helped pile him up with three yards gained. Then McCready, their whippet halfback, came darting wide and Corbett cut him down with another three on a pretty diving tackle. Klein hit on the crossbuck, a foot short of the first down. He was a good smasher, Savage had to admit, as the scout report had noted.

Rossiter went with Klein again for the needed twelve inches, a quick hand-off over guard. He did not get it, because Casper and Fitz and Clawson wedged in and there was suddenly no place for the fullback to go.

The noise from the Hastings stands was like a thunderclap, and a small smile of satisfaction broke the corners of Savage's mouth. The Cavaliers were going to make the Raiders pay cash for every yard. No coach had a right to expect more from his team.

Glass lined up the team in running formation on the 6, faded swiftly, and quick-kicked, a long, low sailer over the heads of the secondary that rolled dead seventy yards downfield.

But Rossiter had power to spare and did not hesitate to spend it. Concentrating inside the tackles and occasionally springing McCready wide, the Raiders marched relentlessly to the touchdown in short thrusts. It took them four plays to get over from the Cavalier 5, but Klein made it by the length of the ball and a moment later it was 7–0.

Crump might have slowed up that drive, Savage told himself, perhaps even stopped it. Certainly his blocking would have helped to get the Cavalier offense moving. But Crump wasn't there, and Travis and Freeman could not find running room against the big blue forwards.

So Glass kicked again and Rossiter substituted for nine of its starters. The difference wasn't noticeable, Savage

171

thought ruefully, as the Raiders mounted another long drive that ended shortly after the second quarter opened with Moreno, the right halfback, knifing into the end zone.

Then suddenly Glass fired long to Whitney, who made a neat running catch on the Rossiter 40. It was the Cavaliers' first real threat, but Rossiter held and Glass kicked once more.

The punt was a short one, but high, and McCready let it go rather than try the catch surrounded by red-shirts. It struck the ground and took a perverse bounce, hitting McCready on the leg and then rolling slowly toward the goal line.

Hearst put McCready out of the way with a wicked block and Maderas fell on the ball just four yards away from the goal line.

Even then, the Raiders made it tough. Glass finally burrowed through a tangle of legs on fourth down, Whitney kicked, and on the scoreboard, at least, it was still anybody's game at 14–7.

But only on the scoreboard. Rossiter was driving again when the half ended, and Rossiter drove with the second half kickoff.

LaCosta's laconic voice checked off the deficiencies, but he knew as well as Savage that personnel, not tactics, held the answer.

"Casper's flagging, Ed. The center's taking him alone. And Mahoney is dead on his feet. They're giving him a bad time with the double-teaming."

"They're putting up an argument, though, aren't they, Sambo?" Savage said it regretfully. "Too bad we don't have three or four more horses, but I can't fault 'em for effort."

He substituted where he could, hoping that the fresh reserves could hang on temporarily. The Raiders banged down to the 10 on sheer power, only to be set back fifteen yards for holding. Klein plowed over tackle to regain eleven of them, but on the next play the quarterback went for the running pass and Hearst got through fast.

He batted the ball and it went straight up in the air. From the side, Chuck Bedolla came with a rush and a leap to pluck it from the waiting hands of Hearst and the Raider quarterback. No one came close enough to touch him on his eighty-five-yard race to the end zone, but he collapsed in exhaustion one stride past the goal line.

Savage got him out of there at once, and Chuck came off breathless, to be almost trampled by joyous teammates as the Hastings rooters stood up and simply yelled. They did not stop yelling even after the infuriated Raiders stormed through to block the try for point.

They can't keep up this stuff, Savage thought, his elation mingling with wonderment. But the exhilarated Cavaliers hurled back the next Rossiter thrust and forced the first Raider punt of the game. And then they stopped another after two first downs when the plucky little Fitzgerald red-dogged Klein on a fullback draw and upended him with six yards lost.

That was all for Fitz; he had played himself out. He came stumbling off the field and Savage met him with the look of a father welcoming a favorite child.

He had to use Murdock to replace him, knowing that if Clawson faltered under the incessant hammering, he had to go down to a third stringer, Warren.

The minutes ticked by, and midway in the fourth quarter fate crooked a finger at the Raiders once more. On fourth down, the Rossiter punter got a bad pass from center, picked it up, dropped it, picked it up again, and tried to run. He had no chance, and there was Hastings in possession on the Rossiter 15.

173

Grimly, the Raiders threw Travis for no gain, batted down two of Glass's throws. There was no course but to attempt a field goal. As a hush settled over the Hastings side of the field, thousands literally holding their breath, Whitney got it away straight and true from the 22. Hastings 16, Rossiter 14. Victory lay in the Cavaliers' grasp.

They could not hold it. Watching with what effort the battered Clawson pulled himself to his feet after each play, Savage had to take him out. Hearst was used up; so was Whitney. They had reached the end of their resources and there was no point in keeping them on the field to be trampled by fresher men.

With the grim assurance of a team that knew it was not going to be denied, the Raiders marched to the touchdown, making five and six yards a play where they had made only three before. Klein, rested through most of the third period, charged across for the score, smashing his way through the clutches of Fairchild and Murdock. Two minutes later it was over.

By the time Savage got back to the dressing room, the newspapermen, including Jake Gledhill, were waiting there in readiness.

"In a few minutes, if you don't mind," Savage said. "I'd like to talk to the kids first."

"It was quite a game, Ed," Gledhill said, and there was admiration in his voice.

"Yes." Savage nodded. "I thought it was a good game —a really good one."

He closed the dressing-room door behind him.

They were a beat-up, heartsick group of youngsters, he thought sadly as he surveyed them. He could see that some were close to tears.

Savage groped for words that would make them under-

174

stand there was no reason for self-reproach, the feeling of failure. They had played to the very limit of their capabilities and lost to a better team. There should be room for a graceful loser, but in the bruised and tired faces he saw only the overwhelming sense of defeat.

So, knowing he could not talk away their bitter disappointment, he made no attempt. Instead, he went quietly from one individual to another with a consoling phrase, a murmured thanks, or a pat on the shoulder. It was all he could do.

Murchison was there, bleak-faced.

"Tough one to lose, Ed," he said huskily.

"We didn't deserve to win it, Cal." Savage knew what the athletic director was thinking — Vince Crump would have made the difference. "We were lucky to be that close. I'm proud of the way the kids fought it out."

"Yes, they put up a good show," Murchison admitted. He forced a smile. "Maybe next year, Ed."

Savage said: "I hope so, Cal. But not with me. I'm resigning."

Murchison's mouth sagged open.

"You're joking!"

"No, I mean it. It's my fault alone, and I'm sorry, Cal. But I've learned I'm in the wrong business and I want out while I still have time to try something else. I don't like leaving a job unfinished, but there are plenty of others who can finish it better than I could. George Breck, for one."

The hurt, uncomprehending look in Murchison's eyes stabbed at Savage, and he was swept by pity. He was fortunate; he could escape. Cal could not.

"I don't believe it," Murchison said dazedly. "To quit for no reason at all, after a season like this one!"

"Reason?" Savage asked gently. "There are plenty, but now isn't the time, Cal. You announce it when you

175

want to. You'll have it in writing Monday morning, and I won't tell the reporters. Which reminds me that they're waiting for me."

The moon had risen by the time Savage and Sam La-Costa left the building and walked slowly toward the former's car. The players had departed; so had a stricken-looking Murchison. To their left, the sweeping curve of the stadium rim was outlined against the star-dotted sky.

"Will you miss it, Ed?"

"I suppose I will. But then I'll think of you, Sambo, trying to teach some left-footed guard the simple facts of football, and I'll know I did the right thing. For me, anyway."

"Doctor Savage." LaCosta rolled the phrase around his tongue. "I hope I never get sick, that's all, if they give you a license."

"They may not," Savage agreed blandly. "I may be around to see you about an assistant's job, after all."

"You'll need references," Sam said, as they reached the car. "Where are you headed now? Home?"

"I'm picking up Sarah for dinner, but I'll drop you off first."

LaCosta grinned at him.

"Much obliged, but I'll walk. I don't want to delay you. I seem to hear the sound of distant bells."

"If you do, you've got a ringing in your ears," Savage growled. "But if you want to walk, walk ahead."

As Savage got into the car, LaCosta began to whistle a wedding march somewhat off key. Reddening, Savage started the engine, then rolled down the window.

"Sam," he said, "don't wait up for me."

LaCosta waved at him, and he put the car in gear and drove off like a man in a hurry.